A NATURAL LIGHT SHOW

A NATURAL LIGHT SHOW

by

Nik Edge

CHAPTER 1

In a canyon above the coast of Los Angeles, where a few tankers slowly plied their way southward towards the docks of San Pedro, a trailer was dissolving, fading from its once bright 1950s military blue to a rusting hulk of 1970s turquoise, brown tears streaking its sides. Beside it, an even more deeply faded hulk of steel, once blue also, a '48 Ford pickup with disintegrating wheel fenders, rested. It was rescued one week earlier, when its owner had simply driven it to the head of the driveway where it met the main road, because the long, snaking driveway was only dirt, turning into a boggy lake when it rained. The consistency of the road had dried into a baked mud.

Twin beams of a Ford station wagon blurred across the weed-choked, hilly property of the trailer, its driver approaching the driveway with minor trepidation. He would have been more alarmed if he had known that he was coming under the increasing suspicion of the LAPD, which did not accept that a hippy/artist type could afford drugs and a decent living space without gainful employment. Naturally, they suspected him of having some connection to the sale of narcotics. His name was Harry, and his red hair was already turning gray, even though he was only in his early thirties. He had commandeered the wagon on the return trip from a party further up in the hills, which afforded a better view of the sprawling blue ocean. His charges were two young boys and their suitably young parents, who were fairly determined to pry Harry away from his periodic bouts of melancholy.

Harry (a.k.a. the Whiskey Freak) had driven them up to the party earlier that night, and was determined to complete the round trip, despite the fact that fog had enshrouded the entire canyon, to the extent that even the normally long-casting orange lights of police boats shadowing the blue haze surrounded tankers a mile below them in the Pacific Ocean could not be seen. His long mane of hair was still damp from a leap into the small outdoor pool, whose bright yellow lights had approximated an early morning sun.

When he had trudged up the driveway, eucalyptus clusters crunched beneath his feet, and the resinous scent thrilled his nostrils. If he had been asked, he would have explained that his smell sensation had always been exceedingly acute.

It was an era when parties did not have to be dignified by a specific occasion. Often a long-anticipated album sufficed, but on this night the unseasonably cool August weather had prompted a canyon dweller to initiate a burst of telephone calls, the wires stringing together a novitiate's survey of the canyon. Harry had hoped that the party hostess would opt for a more toned down atmosphere of jazz, but, instead, it had been practically an atmosphere of melee inspired by the latest rendition of Zeppelin. He had been convinced to dance to the "Hammer of God" momentarily, but was more interested in smelling, as much as inhaling, marijuana. He liked to hint that he was more enthused about potential intoxication instead of its actual effects on his brain.

As Harry navigated, he conducted an interior monologue about the path back to the trailer, a gradual, serpentine, downward slope. "That road the broken arm," he thought. "This one the curvature of the spine." Especially at night, this intoxicated driver equated steering control to groin anatomy: "By God, if I can keep my balls straight, maybe I'll get us through this yet!" Dan had attempted to wrest control upon their exit from the party, but the Whiskey Freak (Harry) had prevailed: "You're too stoned. Couldn't even find your way to the aurora borealis."

"Sure, you're in control, all right, Harry." Dan prodded, resting his long arm on the door sill while the wind whipped through the compartment.

"Of course, man. Because you're a fucking asshole." Harry threw his troublesome hair back with a vigorous shake of his head, noticing a coyote skim through trees at the extreme periphery of his vision. "Some of these damn coyotes are rusty-looking fuckers, just like you, Dan."

"No, you are. And do you realize that your freckles get redder when you drink?" Dan was clearly warming to the ribbing session.

An hour earlier, a flash from the bustling inner courtyard had forced the Whisky Freak to squint. "Foolish photographers adorn the party," he thought. From the corner of his mouth came the minutest intimation of a scowl. He appreciated the sight of breasts jingling behind thin, satiny halter tops. And, somehow, out of a cloudy brain miasma pulsed the universal clarion call: Flash your tits! But it was as if his inner ear was dysfunctioning, or the ballasted core had sunk. Upon what he depended? Heapings of vodka and large, unlit joints and universal truths proclaimed with a bit of ferment, venturing for the immediate future, and beyond. His antennae were poised for the extraterrestrial encounter, or a particularly spry young female caught by his penetrating sight. But something had escaped him that night, which he could not regain. But just as surely as he was drunk he was also mourning something. Not the death of another day but an idea. He did not have the faintest idea what his last conversation had described in the party. He would have to watch the Rockford Files when he got home to find out. "Fry eggs in butter," he thought.

"All aboard." Harry put the station wagon in drive. "This is a practice in pretzel logic. Night blinders down," he declared, switching off the high beams. "Sara, you drove last. Surely, you blind them with more than your beauty."

"Stop, Harry."

"Yeah, serious now," chimed in Dan.

"Sure, kids. Just strap yourselves in and take a nap," Sara suggested.

"I'm too scared to nap," younger brother protested, elbowed in the ribs by elder brother. *Crazy Horse renascent in Charley Horse pain.*

But too late to disturb Dan, looking strained into unnatural calm. " Just stay away from the line divider, Harry."

"Ay, ay, Captain. Hey, any breath mints in case I run into a Smokey?"

"Harry, they don't have the canyon covered yet. And this stretch is the most remote of all the roads through here."

"He thinks he does," younger brother stated.

"Shut up." Older brother was clearly annoyed. "You don't know how to drive."

"See how I float through the corners? How I leave the gas off?" Harry gently indicated.

"You mean, how you control the vehicle?" older brother rejoined.

"His brain is on the skid, guys," remarked Dan.

Harry snickered. "Yeah, then why does it feel so good?"

Dan triggered: "Do you notice the fog?"

"Which one, the one in my brain, or the one in the air?" Harry's hands fumbled for the dry joint that had fallen into the console when he had pulled out the light switch lever.

"Let's not talk about the one in your brain, Harry," Sara forwarded over the play-fighting bellows.

"I'll smack your head like Hank Aaron."

"Yeah, right, I'll twist you into a pretzel."

"Quiet down, Harry's driving!"

"That's what we're afraid of!" chimed in the boys' falsetto, while a rattlesnake snake skirted the tire treads.

"Did you see Dracula?"

"Yeah, in the mirror, because I'm Dracula."

"Hey, don't invoke the devil's name in vain," chortled Harry.

"Or run over any rabbits!" exclaimed Sara.

"Don't worry, guys, I'm a tortoise on the road tonight. No fuzz will take me in tonight. Although the trip seems especially long. Should we just connect it to the seemingly unending one of life?"

The dirt driveway beckoned, because it had not rained.

Harry awoke in the morning with his long-accustomed shiver-shake, and wondered if it is was a signal of epilepsy. He swung his bowlegged, alabaster legs over the loft bed in his studio in Venice Beach and, from long habit, despite there being no sign of an itch, scratched his groin. He bemoaned another evening of sleeping alone, wondering if his antics had shaken off the perking buds of yet another female carnation.

His hands attached to his ears when a bum in the fronting alleyway smashed a night time's supply of liquor bottles against the side of the building. Harry arced the "F" word toward the offender and the "P" word returned forthwith. He suddenly felt desperate to flee his surroundings, but could not settle on a destination until his bony buttocks touched the wiry seat of his VW bus. He sat for at least fifteen minutes, under the spur of nostalgia, trying to collect, and selectively distort, certain past memories.

Weeds tentacled the driveway of the dilapidated, purple Victorian in downtown L.A., reaching across the sidewalk toward the street.

Harry stubbed out a cigarette on the curb, and whistled a quick Irish ditty. He could barely see the mailbox at the edge of the front porch. He hoped the Pineapple (Pina man) was not lurking back there somewhere in the weeds, like the Green Beret he had been. Frijoles smoke wafted from Pina's abode next door. Harry decided he would infiltrate the small jungle, and return with some booty. He felt like a secret agent, or even a soothsayer, touching his right forearm rose tattoo as if it was a divining rod. He surmised it would soon have to be re-colored. "Maybe a touch more of red next time," he finalized after minute inspection.

He kicked aside a bicycle collapsed inside a particularly deep stand of weeds, itching his exposed shins and thighs in the process, and briefly crouched, ears pricked for any warning noises, like a jaguar. The jagged spur of a Coca-Cola bottle peeked up near a bicycle tire and a faded, flower-bedecked album jacket cover rested, bent, twisted, and soggy. Aroma almost a putrid rendition of an unventilated resin booth. He wore a bandanna, but more loosely than a cholo gangster. *El Viejo.* (The old one). Still moved stealthily. Slipped slowly through, as if to forewarn a corpse by bestirring it. Already he could tell that the half-moon had been graffitied over on the garage door. He had no fear of snakes but despised scurrying mice.

A brass rooster weathervane glinted in the corner of his eye, and he briefly halted. *When did I put that on the roof of the studio? But what about that large slab of stained glass leaning against the door? A faithful replication of Jesus. Hey, Zeus. Que pasa?* But a grimace rebelled against the thought of creating **him.** In the image of the prematurely mangy lion, broken down by the absence of his pride. And in absence the throaty, futile roar. Toward the glass slivers. And the circling jackals. Like the small boy trying to lift his bicycle-"Drop it, you little shit. You'll cut yourself and your father will kill me." The boy scurried off. "Don't come back, either, cholito!" he yelled.

Must reach for another medicinal bottle. They had all abandoned it. Why, Sara? Me to the beach and you and the old man and the kids to the canyon. Because when nudists colonized this yard there was hope. Keening on the wind? (chuckling to himself). Real pot-pourri. Zits and mole hairs and bushy pubics for all to see. Even safety pin earrings and diaper man Dan, whose member slipped out anyway while Krazy Kile banged Squaw Woman just out of earshot of the flourishing birds of paradise. Para dice? " Dumb woman," he thought. "Should have left that racist squaw talk behind." All he needed from women was their sex and virtual friendship. No intimate suffocation predicated on love.

He imagined two enormously overheated and overblown balloons courting on the sunken pin-filled cushions of a raggedy old couch in a small trailer in Palm Desert, reading <u>Naked Lunch</u>. Small woman fondling the garden hose and the fluttering of a rogue pigeon among the still smoldering barbecue scraps atop the <u>Life</u> edition of the first moonwalk, its smoke as certain as that of a marijuana bong pipe.

Where is the Pina man? Perhaps he is having trouble locating son Cue Ball? Could he be in hiding in Ensenada, sleeping with a chiquita in his Lowrider?

His mind quickly created a scene of two young Hispanic lovers snuggling inside a car somewhere around the Mexican border. He pictured a stuck armrest the only impediment to their lovemaking, more than Cue Ball ever would have ever guessed, as he cut it out with his switchblade.

"You're an animal," she sighed.

"Claro que si." (But then who would logically allow one hump to prevent another?) So they sweated together through the night, waiting for the shining lights of the Federalistas to interrupt them.

He tripped over an old oil drum. *Hell, when did I dabble in mechanics?* It almost crested its muddy ditch, then fell back. *Emptying fuel of the sordid past. Am I sure I transported the last of my resin barrels to my studio in Venice? Did Chief Longfeather offer his covered wagon for transport? Told him he was shaming his supposed red-faced ancestors(Caesar wore no face paint, at least as much as historians have established).*

Hiccuped. *Should have scarfed one of Jose's chicken tacos. Blessed it with green sauce. But Jose would have bungled it, putting in tiny crushed red peppers for my effrontery. Altogether, a friendly enough chap, sends some compensation back to a family in Mexico, who resort to pig slops.*

He envisioned another dusty Mexican road:

Backwards or forwards, their cars only coasted. Reverse, record the frown on the mustached bandito, aiming a barely operable pistol at an inoperable Model T. Pistolero: "Damn the machines!"

CHAPTER 2

A t the police Rampart division, two miles nearby in downtown Los Angeles, Officer O'Dool saw the name Harry O'Shea while rifling through the umpteenth file on Rudolph Valentino Pina. Occasionally, in between frustrated snorts, he peered through the long, floor to ceiling vertical windows, coated with a fine layer of dirt, which afforded the entire space a dungeon-like atmosphere.

O'Dool was a tanned, stocky man in his early forties neither concerned nor unconcerned about his bulging waistline, a cop with an innate aversion to quick fixes. He turned back to regarding the Pina file, resting his arm on top of the heavy metal file cabinet: Pina was an alleged middleman in the Tijuana-Boyle Heights drug connection, doing business out of a slowly disintegrating Victorian in downtown Los Angeles. Miscellaneous firearms and marijuana found during recent search-and-siezure operations, but the department was after bigger drug fry. *Salacious chiquitas, too (munched on his cheese sandwich). One called La Naranja(orange). And what happened to her younger sister Tangerine? (smacked his fat, pendulous lips).* Talk in the office about creating some divisions called cubicles filtered around him like asbestos dust, while he reached for the greasy paper sack atop the cabinet to gather another cheese sandwich. Who is Harry O'Shea? Reported having been seen speaking to Mr. Pina on numerous occasions. About what? (O'Dool cursed to himself). About cutting a snide neighbor's throat? Or means of drug transport, both in ingress and egress terms? *Must speak to this hippy without being too obvious. Rather than alarm him and Senor Pina with some type of misdemeanor drug charge.* Harry O' Shea had long been only a name, a minor irritant to the narcs, flashing his long, reddish, blonde hair.

Think *back. That party two years ago, the first time he considered that departmental politics might soon lead him to quit. Was said the top cholos and cholas would converge. Festival a la old Olvera Street. Officer Hernandez's first undercover assignment. Wearing that bandana comfortably, along with the flappy chinos and white Converse All-Stars. Hell, the first year of expanded undercover!* Year the annual barbecue on the beach in the shadow of the crumbling Santa Monica pier erupted with Beach Boys blaring, everyone in Hawaiian get-ups, women treated as everyone's wife, although every couple eventually went home together, intact.

Sergeant York's white convertible Cadillac was puked in, the poor imitation muscle car, fused by Pep Boys. *Could not trust speed with a prostituted mechanic plugging for the mighty corporation.*

York had exited in a fury, spewing invective at Lieutenant Smith's Corvette and Chief Bender's Mustang. Comments to the effect that Bender was ruining the top-flight Pina case, the case upon which his promotion to the DEA depended. O'Dool's argumentative wife Mary, who had been badgering him about more money to refurbish their house, was possessed by flower print furniture blues: "How am I supposed to entertain guests with an outdated plaid sofa?" Later, she was unmoved by his bar-talk, vodka-splashed amorous dash, making him sleep alone on the musty couch.

O'Dool's desk, a hulking gray metal contraption with slowly failing hinges, was the terminus of joker's platform. Every crude joke deposited there at the close of day: What's the difference between a monkey and a woman? You can spank your monkey whenever you want, but you can't so much as touch your wife. Some unknown person actually crossed it out with a leaky fountain pen and wrote "Stupid Existential Joke" *(Henceforth, all black jokes to be excised from the public record).*

O'Dool thought the nervy script perfectly fit Detective Fitzsimmons. Like the quirky private dick. Eternal bachelor confidently sailed the unpredictable, but rarely unpleasant waves of female sexuality. Favored a porkpie hat and a frenchified, dandy-thin mustache. Claimed he once posed in a cigarette advertisement with a Moll-on-the-Floss-Menthol girl, straight from Hollywood High.

O'Dool himself was more concerned about purchasing virgin property in Laurel Canyon due west of Hollywood Hills, and building one of those wood structures on gigantic stilts in order to star gaze with his telescope.

"Find your own nebulae" (his father speaking?). O'Dool thought, "That damn strict academic, with his hermit's nest in northern California." As a kid, O'Dool stole strawberries from neighbor Old Man Sam, who riposted, "So you're the damn future of law enforcement?"

Dad's dinner guests were often Jesuit priests who liberally poured from red wine bottles while virtually cursing their poor church provisions. "Damn crooked card players, too," O'Dool thought.

"Who wants a chili dog while I'm out?" No one responded. Rookie trying to score some points. A transfer from San Fernando Valley. Unfortunately an expert on Reseda (not Hollywood) Boulevard. Childs was his name. Drove a Dodge Cougar, the distinct poor man's hot-rod, as if women would reward him for his moxie alone. Chubby, he was called. Officers claimed he was so stopped-up with frankfurters that he could no longer properly defecate. Reason he broke wind like breathing and drank Pepto Bismols as if they were bottles of Pepsi. He would return to find O'Dool's terse handwritten message scrawled on the back of a torn envelope: "Reopen the Harry O'Shea file."

Harry's friend Dan had a long, thin build, the wiry type that lent itself to physical pursuits. But his chief quality consisted in a charismatic energy that required no definition beyond his narrow frame, a simplicity that befit his old, yet functioning vehicle in Venice.

The '48 Ford pick-up, fenders burned rust orange at the seams of the brown body, climbed the Pacific Avenue hill. Dan watched the bed through the rearview mirror as he climbed, unsure about the safety status of the six foot red resin piece that was comforted by thick blue moving blankets. He smirked at the downturned jaw of his own visage just as he applied the brakes at the behest of the faded red Stop sign. Shoved the gearshift into first and executed a right turn, palm trees on either side another cushion. Special matt under his backside to protect from bursting springs. *Squirrely wire snakes*. WW II army green issue toolbox to the right at his feet. His Dad's relic. Southwest Pacific. Past the alleyway foxholes of bad drug deals and cheap, quick action. Like Vietnam's Charlie's Angels. Too sweet for The Shit, but Nixon's re-election campaign mired in it. Then descended a different hill. Coasted in neutral. Barely consulted the brakes. Enjoyed brief shade. Past the demonic heat of that corner house at Rose Avenue that periodically hosted murder. Repainted after each installment of mayhem, now a bleached yellow.

Levi's short-shorts, roller derby queens glared at his truck as they rolled past, down to the boardwalk. What kind of yokel truck was that to drive? Esp. here in the city of Charlie's Angels? (in his excitement he grinded the truck's gear shaft). She reached to pull part of the abbreviated pants out of her expansive crack, throwing one buttock slightly out of whack.

Too much action on the weekend. His bastion the red brick studio. A downtown transplant, when the city thought it could produce another industrial area on the shores. But shipping remained south in San Pedro. With Mao Zedong fading in China, a larger wave of illegal Chinese immigrants desperately gambled with their lives, and perished in steel cold bilious filth. Perhaps one "lucky" soul able to one day run his own establishment without the interference of rackets.

His alleyway was choked with garbage. Pulling out his garage keys he noticed the bum Tom resting just within the limits of confinement underneath the dumpster. In a bright-checked bathrobe and bear slippers. *The bum's everlasting body chill.* Dan rolled the heavy door to the right and Tom slightly budged. Dan left the light momentarily off. He bemusedly eyed the old Ford pick-up behind him. Tom nodded once, then resumed his catatonic position.

Dan returned to the relief of old canvasses hung everywhere, images like some Native American sign language. *But what import and what shape?* He still reworked them. Chief Longear might have proposed a sun dance studio with his Sun Goddess blooming on the rose-petaled floor. Slats of the dormer windows were rusty and the utility sink was dripping and Tom was blithely moaning. Scrap wood spread across the floor like the detritus of fallen trees, each anchored onto his collective psyche.

He turned on the table saw, and with ease cut the large pieces into smaller versions of their grain. But the radio had to be activated to gain stride (Harry always said he could chop-saw while executing the Texas

Two Step). Smaller scraps deposited in a large cardboard box. Discordant ice cream truck music drifted through the still supine form of Tom, filtering into the studio.

It is as if he was engaged in cutting trinkets for Santa. He pulled out the sketchbook directly afterward. Thumbed back to adolescent drawings. When he had that Snoopy Dog artiste on his hot rod driver's side door, now, in retrospect, an image of his sheepdog-wolfhound mix dog Danny. But now his ken was simply the Aztec Warrior. *Must pull the monolilth out of the truck bed with Tom's scant assistance beside the throbbing pulse of the Doors' "Break On Through."*

In a bar off Main St., only one mile from Harry's old downtown property, where Bunker Hill dove to its premature end, and the rails to the defunct Angel's Flight rail ride were still visible through weeds and broken glass, the double saloon doors parted for a patron beset by a caffeine-induced migraine. O'Dool did not notice a large head with a crew cut head staring at his back. Afterall, what did he have to fear from an old drunk?

O'Dool perceived the flame abruptly. Grabbed the arm before it could pull back the brandished lighter. Watched the bar mirror for a sign from the downturned face. The glint of the gold Zippo was faint.

"When did you start sneaking up on people?"

"When I realized I couldn't scare them anymore." Jones, a former cop, rapped a ringed finger on the walnut bar top.

O'Dool began to twist the arm, then rested it on the bar like a cord of wood. It barely twitched.

"Hey, where have you been?" O'Dool appreciated the old black-and-white photo portraits of local Golden Gloves boxing champions.

"Around. Couldn't stay retired at home. I know you wish I'd just stay away, at least preferably so?" Jones rapped his finger on the bar again.

"Preferably so, huh? No, preferably, I'd like you to sit next to me at this bar as much as possible. Preferably I'd like you to work on the goddamn O'Shea case. And, preferably, you could convince the chief that it is a waste of his, my, and the entire department's time. Pina's so small-time I feel I'm on some Cub Scout mission."

Jones smirked and scratched his chin. "Hey, slow down. Let me get seated first, bartender, get me a straight whiskey and a beer back. I'm constipated every day, but I guess yours are still tougher. By the way, you shouldn't have grabbed my arm. The flame could have singed your eyebrows."

"Don't threaten me, all right? You're something, Jones. If you're not an old fart I'm drunk."

Jones slapped him on the back. "You are. But your chief used to be my partner, and even then he was too political. But, hey, don't rush to the conclusion that I'm judging him."

"Yeah, every man has a greedy wife at home to support. Right?" O'Dool grimaced at his own image in the spider-cracked mirror.

"Hey, you're drinking too fast. That's why it all tastes so bitter."

O'Dool shrugged. "I'm just worried about freaks, foreign and domestic."

Jones' shoulders tightened around his own neck. "Bullshit. You're kidding me. There's something else you want to say. But then, like they say, unspoken words are always the more truthful ones."

"What kind of talk is this, anyway? You were always-what's the word-too philosophical for your own good." O'Dool was focusing on a particular portrait, of a black boxer baring his filed teeth.

Jones harrumphed. "Now you're sounding like the prick." He rubbed a surface scar on his right cheek.

"I never used such a word, Jones. Might have thought it, but, hey, you still live in Studio City?"

"Yeah, but who cares? They wanted to give me some rent rebate for pool and security work. As if I was desperate to be an authority figure. People never realize I never felt comfortable, you know?" He gulped large liquid and reached for the peanut dish.

"No, asshole, a gun. That whole supposed civil weapon and sidearm jargon irked me from the get-go. Those words make me think of a nightstick, for crying out loud. When I think of weapon or sidearm, I think of something that could be shoved up your ass, not something that can fire a small projectile completely through somebody." Jones' neck cords tightened.

O'Dool shrugged. "Never thought much about it myself, Jones, but sidearm is almost like sidekick, right?" O'Dool was wondering if the boxer in the portrait was African, and that that was why his teeth had been filed, or, on the other hand, if it was yet another example of the type of brute ego that had to reside in a pugilist's soul.

"Sure, sure, but, barkeep, another round over here." He reached for a red plaid rag and mopped his forehead. "But back to your predicament, which is more interesting." Jones looked slightly pained.

"How so?" O'Dool's last thought was about how the teeth procedure was done on the black boxer without damaging the roots.

Jones grimaced. "Don't be so cheeky, all right? This Pina business."

O'Dool leaned forward. "Fuck Pina, all right? I mean, the guy is nothing more than a small time crook."

Jones held up his right index finger. "But they think somehow he's linked to the big time, right? You don't have to tell me more. They want a t.v. series to be made about their huge bust. But why fight the Feds? I should know. One of my oldest pals survived years of the DEA."

O'Dool settled back. "Yeah. And too many rookie cops raised on Dragnet. Don't realize that no single cop is treated with any special respect. Too many alcoholics and wife beaters."

Jones laughed. "Well, I see not much has changed since I retired. Immoral cops, if not corrupt ones."

O'Dool had a single peanut in his palm, which he was trying to squish with his fingers. "Now you're sounding Christian! What if I was to say that I beat my wife?" O'Dool had clearly been effected by the fighting atmosphere of the bar.

Jones raised to the tips of his elbows. "You bastard."

O'Dool patted his shoulder. "Come on. It's too easy and fun to upset you. It's good you don't wear the badge anymore, with that quick temper of yours."

Jones once again comfortably settled on his stool. "I could do something about it, but I choose not to. An old crank like myself has to watch himself." Jones swirled the whiskey in his glass.

"Evidently. But let's just keep drinking until Friday afternoon turns to Friday evening." O'Dool returned to the portrait of the black fighter with the razor sharp teeth. He thought that it had been too long since he had seen a prizefight in person.

Billy kicked dirt in the blonde canyon. Spat in it. Wielded his stiff blandishing hand like a blade while the blonde brothers rubbed their eyes, still tired from the previous night, and the exciting drive home, with the talk of vampires and snakes. The older brother had a denser mop of hair, a dirty blonde, while the smaller one had a thinner patina of milky white. Meanwhile, beyond thick scrubs of weeds, Dan wielded a hose in bathing his rust-streaked pickup, while three dogs battled to snap at the stream of water. He occasionally paused to watch Billy and his boys' antics down slope.

Billy spoke softly to the mesa, his thick, long black hair hanging over his face like a mask. Juggling twigs and oak leaves. Sara could see him and her boys from her porch one hundred yards away, sitting under the trailer porch awning with a dog-eared poetry book. She could see the clouds of dust generated by his grading feet, and the flurry of one short arm. "Hum," she thought, eyes flitting back and forth, from word and paper to flesh and sound, because he was speaking.

"Forgive these stupid pale faces. They don't know what to do. I'll speak for them, because they are wrong. They have lost the spirit. I could throw dirt in their eyes, or smear their faces with shit, but that would not do. They are silent, but they are ashamed of their dirty race. I think they should burn up their Kid Colt comic books as punishment. They need to be cleansed before we can become blood brothers. I won't let their impure blood stink up this holy place." As he spoke, older brother was busy tying a slip knot from string. "I will show them mercy even though they don't deserve it. Let us just take our time, and pass around the holy cola water." He uncapped the freezing mixture and took four large gulps. "I have tasted and like it fine, Great Spirit, so I can now pass it around to these whiners. While they have theirs, know that I am called to wisdom by the holy worm, the one which the sacred eagle swallows. I eat the worm and spit fire."

Gestures folded into premature character around his dark eyes, his message vested in flailing arms. Sara smiled at no mention of knives, and avidly continued reading verse.

"Help these boys. Even though I'm a man, I can only do so much. My Mom made me a man young, so I can speak the truth. Let them hear themselves. That's all I can ask for. All these Palefaces can see now is black, in their blond canyon."

Sara returned to pondering Sexton: A *snake in the grass, with smoke wafting upward, contrabanding an essence of poesy, flirting with redemption; tendrils of smoky exhalations merging with the dissipated exhaust of Winchester rifles.* Sara in cut-off Levi's shorts, flip flops, and red winged sunglasses. She was favoring sweetened iced tea and the pleasure of smoothing an escaped black lock back to its property behind the ear, while reshaping her own words within the notes of Paul Simon trilling off the trailer steps…"Love Me Like A Rock."

From a distance, Sara regarded Billy, then Billy's mother Maude sitting beside her. *When was the last time the straight, jet black hair was properly reset through applications of shampoo*? Instead, Maude's maladroit set of shaking fingers had tangled it. She regarded Sara with underwater eyes: "You look dark. Yes, gosh, you do. Are you one of us?"

"No, I'm just part Italian."

"You don't look greasy, though." She hacked into a plaid handkerchief.

"No."

"Well, Italian starts with "I" and so does Indian. You know, I'm glad Petey left Billy and me. You see me drinking and all, but what self-respecting man calls himself Petey? Should have called him Peep instead, he had such a small pecker. I know, you're thinking it's sad, not funny. True, he was a sad case, but the reservation was killing me. You wouldn't believe it, but I drink less now than I did then." She looked outside, but beyond Billy and his friends, into the unknown distance.

Greasy hands reached for the vodka bottle, tight-capped on the edge of the vinegary couch. Chapped lips clamped around a gnawed cigarette. The bright beads wound into long strands of hair clicked together helter-skelter.

"Hey, Sara?" Her eyes had hardened once more.

"Yeah?"

"Kids are a bitch, aren't they?"

"Well, yes, but…"

"But? No. You know my heart is not mean, woman. I mean how much they take, and take from a woman, until there is nothing left of her. I wish I had a turquoise necklace for every time I regretted Billy, but no, don't get me wrong, more times than not I feel grateful for him."

Billy whirled and hopped on one foot at a time, and the raised dust flew into the paleface eyes. There was resultant sneezing and coughing. Then Billy pulled out his Buck knife, and slashed at the airborne circles of dust.

CHAPTER 3

C hief Bender had badgered O'Dool all morning about tailing drug dealers. Finally, after his cheese sandwich supply had been exhausted, and his strolls through the bleak concrete courtyard had garnered him nothing except a burgeoning headache due to the blaring sun, he had relieved the community refrigerator of the last two cans of Tab, and loosened his suspenders in preparation for an exit, his underarms itching with sweat. He had always considered himself the prototypical beat cop, the kind that was intimate with specific neighborhoods, but during Bender's reign it seemed that working as pseudo-narcs for the DEA was their chief concern. O'Dool was chagrined, but realized that it was more lucrative, in the sense that drug convictions were more numerous and easier to prosecute than homicide cases. O'Dool figured that Bender had been lining his own pockets with kickbacks from various schemes, but had no specific ideas.

O'Dool turned left onto Venice Boulevard, and horns blared as the signal light flashed red, and the glare of a screeching-to-a-halt Chrysler Plymouth bumper struck his windshield. He kept accelerating, because the Ford Pinto was too many car lengths ahead, although he was able to scramble for the dial of the radio when the first bars of Tiny Tim crackled through the dashboard speaker. So it behooved him to accelerate through another red light, whereupon more screeching tires signaled him to arrest his reverie. "Stop your whining. Just do the fucking job," he said aloud to himself. He gained ground, passing a Volkswagen bus with a faded Peace Sign bumper sticker and an indescribable jalopy with balding tires and a bald head at the controls. "Old Conehead," he said aloud.

Even from a distance, the suspect's head was unnaturally large, but not round. Instead, it was elongated, like a giant egg. "Huge twisted brain," O'Dool said aloud. With a mop of curly blond hair on top. O'Dool surmised that the hair cushion was a preventative for police cruiser- carhood- concussive syndrome, because his arrest record was lengthy, if only misdemeanor-rich. "Dopey freak." Suspect's name? Legal: Larry Smith. Streetwise: Pippen. Only under the severest duress would he cop to the fact that his supposed name was a complete fabrication, unsupported by any legal documentation. "Hippies die hard," he said aloud.

The Pinto floated to the right and left, but stayed within its lane. O'Dool was encouraged, and maneuvered directly behind it, easing along in the mid-afternoon of sparse traffic. "So fucked up he won't notice me," he thought. He already considered it a dead-end assignment, but he could not directly countermand the order. Aromas from Juan's taco stand assailed him, and he almost braked. "Screw this assignment," he thought. He imagined Maria waving to him as he rushed past, pouting with her red lipstick, and her surly brother Pedro giving him the middle finger with the bulb of a jalapeno pepper stuck to it like a green light bulb.

O'Dool braked to turn right, but the Pinto came to a complete halt, even though the light was still green. Horns blared, but still the car did not move, the head not turning in either direction to investigate. But when a stocky man strode ahead from his Chevy truck, and was halfway to the seemingly stalled car, Pippen pressed the gas. "Shit head smartass." O'Dool ignored the irate man yelling at each car that passed him as he made his way back to his truck. He laid back again as the Pinto led him through a neighborhood of faded crabgrass lawns, small houses with metal awnings shading the fierce August sun. There was a pair of legs sticking out from underneath a jacked-up Ford Fairmont at the first Stop sign intersection, and the Pinto stopped once again. The head turned slowly, mechanically, and, even from his removed position, O'Dool could hear the Pinto engine revving, saying, "your engine might be fucked, but mine is fine, thank you." The two legs emerged from the chassis, followed by a white tee shirt torso and a pin head with a buzz cut, slightly shaking on its thin stem. The man shook his head as the Pinto idled away, and when O'Dool's car passed, he was already rolling back underneath on his dolly.

"Fucky funny, Ronald McDonald," O'Dool said aloud. He imagined the floppy head bouncing off the trunk of a car, leaving a quick, red kiss of Ronald McDonald lips. Again, he had to arrest the reverie, as he was reminded of Maria's sumptuous lips.

The Pinto pulled into the driveway of another nondescript house, except for the presence of iron bars over each window. O'Dool parked on the other side of the street, a half block down, and reached into the glove compartment for a warm cheese sandwich. He chewed and swallowed and watched Pippen move slowly and deliberately, in his wide yellow terry-cloth shirt, Levi's, and Van's sneakers, unclip a huge circle of keys from a side loop, and, without hesitation, match each plastic color to its proper bolt lock, and in a sudden spasm of quick, intense activity, unlock all six. "Eccentric fuck," he thought. O'Dool sensed that he had been spotted, so he did not apprehend any meaning from the fact that Pippen closed the door behind him without once looking back.

O'Dool waited fifteen minutes, bothered by the lack of a breeze. He pulled away, already creating a report in his head: "Trailed suspect. No contact. Erratic. But dangerous?" He underlined the question mark. "What do the Feds want with types like Pina, O'Shea, and Pippen?" It irked him to reflect that, in the event that the case mushroomed into something of "federal interest," the Feds would force the LAPD to turn over its entire files, and capitalize on the painstaking work done by cops like him.

Harry, in his Volkswagen bus, took little notice of O'Dool passing him in pursuit of the Pinto. He sipped from a warm can of beer resting between his knees. A block beyond where the other two vehicles turned, he recollected himself, and turned in the opposite direction. "You're going to the dentist, idiot," he said aloud to himself. He braked to examine his leonine face in the mirror, noting how scraggly and unkempt his beard appeared. Picking and smoothing through the red-and-white, hairy mass, he found old bits of Spam entangled, and a bit of dried blood, which he could not relate to his present condition. He smoothed his hair as best as he could, and popped a breath mint. "Smooth and easy now." Finishing the beer in two long gulps, he threw it over his shoulder, and it shattered the sound of the idling engine. "Shit. Must be two hundred cans back there." He watched a housewife, somewhat large but curvy, bend down to pick up her paper. "Good hams, ma'am," he appreciatively remarked.

Willing himself to put the van in gear, he still examined himself in the mirror. Nothing surprised him, except for the scab on his right earlobe. "Crazy Mary took a bite." He wondered why the abandoned house downtown, with its millions of snaky weeds, kept calling to him. When he awoke in the morning, his half-dream state told him that he had left something invaluable behind before he moved to Venice. *A first edition Andy Warhol print? Or a raw diamond? Or, perhaps, a*

woman's still slightly scented silk kerchief? Stuck in a fallen cactus?
How many cholos jumped the fence and trampled the garden?

He crossed Century Boulevard, recalling how his brakes had failed
at the same spot two years previous, and he was searched and grilled by
a cop for close to fifteen minutes. It had not helped matters when he
had given the exchange some heat:

"Sir, are you carrying any narcotics on your person?"

"Well, sir, could you first define 'narcotics'?"

"Sir, could you please step out of the vehicle."

"Had trouble drawing out that robotic cop," he thought. The end
result? A benumbing court room, next to the overpriced soda machine
refilled once a day in the summer heat, abandoned by a malfunctioning
swamp cooler, its ribs in similar pattern to the graying hair of the
scrawling woman clerk. "Was I hallucinating?"

He had forced the most stiff, judicial language to issue from his
scratchy voice box. "Your honor, I have the bill for the brake work
here. And, if it would please the court…"

He decided on a delaying action, a quick bar stop at Pat's, to cool
his head. Even with the windows down, the hot desert air parched his
throat. He had finished his last beer, and espied a giant Seagram's
advertisement atop the old post office building at the corner of La Brea.
A huge patch of corroded paint had flaked off, and had gamely attached
itself to the Seagram girl's nose halfway down the façade.

Halfway across the street, Harry stopped, and walked back to the van. He pulled the keys out of the ignition, and did not notice the partial blotter pad of acid on the passenger side footboard.

When he opened the door, he already felt cooled. He took an empty stool at one end of the bar nearest the door, at furthest remove from an old-timer at the other end near the men's room. *Bar etiquette*.

"What will it be, old-timer?" The bartender had the type of greasy beard that almost prompted Harry to ask if he had ever used it as an egg beater.

"Do I really look old?" Harry enquired.

The bartender exhaled in a prolonged fashion. "Yeah, I can tell you dyed your beard red."

"In that case, a whiskey sour, and a beerback."

"You okay?" the bartender cocked his head slightly to the side.

"Okay. So I look fucked. What else is on tap?"

"Well, sir, you mean beer, or the television?"

Harry coughed. "Come on. Don't put on airs. What I meant was, is there anything besides me looking fucked? I'm paranoid enough as it is."

"Since you put it that way, no. There is nothing else to you."

Harry guffawed. "Okay. Let me take a seat now." He returned the flat stare of his fellow patron, and just caught the corner of the stool with his right buttock. "Damn, that hurts."

"Come again, sir?"

"My ass, my lack of an ass that rubs on a bone. God did not endow me with a seat cushion."

"That's a shame, because they'll have to put your ass in a sling that way."

Harry tittered. "Don't get funny with me, barkeep."

"No, I wouldn't go funny on you." The bartender said it with an expansion of his chest, as if pleasantly surprised by his own wit.

"Okay. That's enough. Let's talk about that pissed-off guy across the way. What ate his guts?" Harry blurted.

"Jimmy there? Well, he fancies himself a real patron, you know? I mean, he is such a regular he likes to think he is a kind of part owner. You know, likes to suggest the liquor content of mixed drinks…"

"And you?" Harry tore his eyes off a buxom brunette Coors Light girl poster hanging above the bar mirror near the ceiling.

"Oh no. I just run the day show for old Mr. Spiegelman."

"That's what I thought. Hey, give me another shot, all right? I'm on a roll now." Harry threw the peace sign at his fellow patron, who did not respond.

"Okay. Bottom's up."

Harry scratched at the cleft of his chin. "You know, I thought I heard that name Spiegelman from somewhere."

"Did you?" The bartender clinked glasses in soapy water up to his elbows, and gave a few cursory glances at the old patron.

"Yeah. I heard he was a patron of the arts, a real investor in creativity."

"Well, all I know for sure is that he collects furniture antiques." The bartender put his elbows up to the top soap suds in the commercial sink.

Harry leaned forward. "Do you think he collects art?"

"You mean paintings?" A huge soap disengaged from its soup and attached to his fat chin.

"Well, kind of. But I'll save you the trouble of asking. I'm an artist myself, a synthesizer of forms."

"Come again?" He blew through his large mouth, and the soap bubble fled.

Harry cleared his throat. "I like to think I combine the best of certain elements, that's all. Sculpture, painting, science, philosophy, color, shade, angle, form."

"Right." The bartender walked down to the other end and waved off the old-timer. "No. I didn't forget you. But maybe you should slow down, Shavers. It's very early and your head is already caved in."

"So? What do I care? Why do you want to talk to some hippie like that? He probably rides a Harley and slits throats for fun." His laugh was more of a choked-off croak.

"Don't get nasty, Shavers. If you can't calm yourself I'll have to eighty-six you. Now, you don't want that, right?" He turned on his heels.

Harry ignored the hard stare of the crotchety old-timer, and pulled a bill out his wallet as the barkeep approached him.

"Barkeep, I have to get going. But I want to talk to you later about Mr. Spiegelman. Maybe I'll stop by tomorrow. I'd really like to know what kind of art he patronizes."

The bartender paused, as if unwilling to continue speaking. "You think you can sell him something of yours?"

"Maybe." Harry poked at a piece of food debris between his incisors.

"Uh huh. I'll think about that between now and the next time we talk. I have to tell you, though, that Mr. Spiegelman is very picky."

Harry stood. "That's a good sign, barkeep. Have a good day, then." When he saw the acid tablets on the VW bus floorboard, he snatched them up, and ate them like dissolving breath mints, washing them down with warm beer.

Two hours later, Harry pulled a suction hose out of his mouth, and blurted, "Hey, doc, what kind of drugs will I get for this?" His arms already felt unnaturally heavy, and his face tingled. There was no response, and two pairs of arms descended on him like giant pliers, and forced the hose back in. "Sadists," he thought. "Baby killers, I'll…"

Eyes opened to a hand turning thread in his still gaping mouth. "Spinner of yarns?" he thought. Fingernails painted with gold stars and clowns. "Am I hallucinating?" A clownish smear of red lipstick on fat lips, around huge buck teeth. "Nurse Charity?" There was a faux pop artist print on the wall, depicting a profusion of ballooned condoms.

"You be a good boy, Mr. O'Shea. Or else I'll make you watch me floss between every tooth of this skeleton."

"Bloody angles," he said aloud.

"Dr. Zeitgeist told me to tell you he is disappointed. He thought he could extract more gold from your pulled teeth." A voice cackled through the operating room speaker. "Beware, Mr. O'Shea is a threat to himself."

"Help me, nurse."

"What is it?" She kept at a safe distance, blowing him kisses (so he thought) under a hairy upper lip.

"She must be hairy all over," he thought.

"I have to go to the restroom." Harry struggled to sit up, fighting the restraining arms.

"I'm under strict orders, Mr. O'Shea."

"Help me get up!" He was reclined at a steep angle, so he had to catapult himself out of the seat.

"Well, in that case,"

"Just shut up, and help me to the bathroom, okay?" He feigned a momentary faint, and let his face drop into her ample bosom. Soft bliss. "That's it. Yes." His face was forcefully (not harshly) pushed away. "Okay. I've got it from here."

An hour later, Harry was still in the bathroom, mentally taking note of the lime-green walls and pink floorboards. He had urinated repeatedly, but that was beside the point. There was a lack of provocative magazines, and the antiseptic smell was overpowering. He had demanded to speak privately to Doctor Zeitgeist, but was told that he had gone home early, for his private yoga lesson. So he spoke cryptically while he listened to the hurried footfalls outside the locked door. "Perhaps if you were to bring a beer I could talk honestly," or, "my psychiatrist is out of town, but another might do for the time being." In fact, he had never consulted a psychiatrist.

"Mr. O'Shea, could we speak about resolving this situation?" To Harry, it sounded like "dissolving."

"Who are you? You sound like a horse with laryngitis." *Mr. Ed.*

"I'm doctor Jeffers. Have not made your acquaintance before. But I'm concerned about all of this office's patients."

Lengthy pause. *Ass kisser. Mama's boy. Make him wait.*

"Mr. O'Shea, I am concerned about you. You have not responded to simple questions. Do you know, is there specifically anything wrong?"

"Harry?" *Another voice.* "This is Bruce. Cut out the crap, or I'll have to cut your balls off."

"Bruce? Where did you come from? And whose side are you on anyway? I thought you were still locked up for unnatural relations with your dogs."

Bruce punched the door once, firmly, but not too violently. "My side. But what made you think I'd be happy about you hogging the men's bathroom?" Bruce had once been deemed not suitably violent enough to join the Hell's Angels, even though he had the gruff manner and huge physique that they favored. Ever since, he had taken out his frustration on furniture, in hopes of some day ridding himself of the pain and embarrassment.

"Hey, asshole, how was I supposed to know you were here?"

"You know, you're getting nasty now. I'm warning you, I'll call Patty so she can bring my tools over."

Harry chuckled. "What are you now, Mr. Maytag Man? Listen, you'll need my cooperation to remove the doorknob."

"You wouldn't dare."

"Oh yeah? I dare you to call Patty then." Harry's voice was virtually triumphant.

"Hell dog!" Bruce hollered.

"Rictus face!" Harry returned.

"Gentlemen! Gentlemen!" *Not Jeffers again.* "We do not want to call the police, Mr. Bruce, and it seems you are only exacerbating the situation."

Bruce's voice minutely softened. "What do you exactly mean by exacterbating?" You're supposed to be a dentist, not an English professor."

Harry riposted, "You know what it is, Bruce? You're just plain stupid."

"Hell Dog!"

"Rictus face!"

Harry's voice became cutting. "You're prepared to take responsibility for whatever happens? Huh, Jeffers? Even with Dr. Zeitgeist gone?"

Jeffers cleared his voice, his hands in his deep, front pockets. "Mr. O'Shea, he expressly told me to take charge with him absent from the office."

"I want him back! Bruce, hold the cops at bay for me when I kick the door down."

"Okay, Mr. O'Shea. It's time…" Jeffers feet tapped nervously in place.

"No. I'll come out in another half hour. That's about the time it will take for the police to arrive anyway. You'll waste your time, Mr. Jeffers, on a telephone call."

Bruce's voice was suddenly apologetic. "It's too late, Harry. I already told him to call."

"Bullshit, Bruce."

"You'll see. It's too late to call it off."

"Bullshit." Harry's voice was loud once more.

"Well, anyway you look at it, you're going to look like a royal asshole, and…"

"Rictus face!"

"Hell dog!"

"Okay, gentlemen. I'll meet the squad car outside, and call the whole show off."

Harry giggled. "Whole show, huh? Right, good fellow. Just wait until I come back for my gingivitis treatment."

A Nurse's voice: "Dr. Jeffers, Mr. Morris wants to know how much longer he has to wait."

"Okay, tell him we have a situation and offer to have some food and drink delivered to him, if he so desires."

Suddenly, Harry sounded pleasant. "Yeah, and get Bruce and me a small flask of whiskey while you're at it."

Bruce harrumphed. "Speak for yourself. A Pink's chili bacon dog would be good right about now."

Harry snickered behind the door. "You trying to draw me out now, Bruce?"

"No. I hope you starve in there, Harry."

Jeffers' voice was renewed with confidence. "Oh, by the way, Mr. O'Shea, when we called in, you were reported by name."

Cruel bastard. "Christ! What do you have against me anyway, Jeffers? Is it just because I had a nervous reaction to Novocain?"

"I doubt the veracity of that, Mr. O'Shea. But you didn't do any damage in there, did you?"

"No. Just ate some rolls of toilet paper, but I've still got ten minutes to go. Hey, Bruce. Bruce?"

"Bruce has gone away. He finished his appointment."

"Good. Never really liked the bastard, even when we were buddies."

"Dr. Jeffers?"

"Yes, Mindy?"

"The police would like to speak to you."

"Hey, doctor, let me speak for myself. Tell them it was a big mistake, a misunderstanding. And, if it weren't for Bruce...." He heard the receding footfalls, and imagined subdued sirens and blandished badges. Momentarily, he thought about interloping, but sat back down, checking his watch. Beyond the door, he envisioned nothing more than a full whiskey glass in a cool, dark bar with dusty mirrors.

CHAPTER 4

L aurel Canyon had an apartness from the city, its narrow, winding roads containing shaded bungalows reminiscent of medieval European villages. Its elevation allowed for breezes that could not exist in the building-saturated flats, and it was difficult to find a lengthy stretch of road not dominated by shade. It was a time, however, when building permits were plentiful, and cheap, presaging a boom that would begin to constrict the notion of city separation.

In the hills of Laurel Canyon, Dan, who always appreciated the drive from canyon to canyon, approached the construction site foreman, the framing hammer bouncing off his hip. He walked downhill, and, as he approached the top of the rise, he could see more than a few fresh foundations being prepped or poured directly downwind. One tractor busily scooped up dirt at the first curve in the road, its engine breaking the early morning stillness. The foreman, Ed, of a short and slightly bulky build, sipped a cup of coffee, slightly shrugging in his jacket. He turned around slowly.

"Morning, Dan."

"Morning, Ed."

"You always show up on time." There was the hint of an annoyance in his measured voice. "Sometimes you're even early."

Dan, always unsure of small talk, responded somewhat awkwardly, "That's true. I guess unless you make a point of showing up on time..." He admired the way the morning light reflected off the tractor.

"You don't have to finish. It's just that I'm used to having some time alone every morning."

Dan was a little nonplussed by the word "partner," but only momentarily. "Okay, you don't have to finish."

Ed started to smile, but it turned to a frown. "You might as well just show up about a half hour later. Don't worry, you'll get full day's pay, I've just got some business to do on my own sometimes. I get a little jumpy, I guess."

"Okay. That's fine with me." Again, Dan felt that there was something odd persecuting Ed, but he could not begin to identify it.

"You know, Dan, do you ever wake up and feel like a stranger to yourself?"

"Sure. I just hope that I feel like that less and less. That's all one can hope for, I guess." Dan was beginning to feel mechanical, and pressured at the same time.

Ed's posture slightly relaxed. "Right. It's just that I kind of hate this job. Do you ever feel that what you were meant to do isn't exactly what you like, it's just what you simply have to do?"

Dan was uncomfortable with the confession, but did not show it. "I guess so. Have to fool yourself, I guess."

Ed sipped his coffee, and stretched his right arm over the canyon. His left foot tapped on the ground, as if to follow the cadence of his thoughts. "I hate it when I'm assigned something, Dan, especially when it's barely within my powers to accomplish. Like this site. They've given me a strict timetable, and I don't know if I can meet it." Yet, deep inside, he was thinking about a man named Bender, and the demands he was making on him. He thought to himself, "How did I let myself get mixed up with this?"

"I think you've got the crew to do it," Dan responded, as if it was a test of his own mettle.

Ed concurred: "I sure hope so. Because, well, my future work might depend on it."

"How so?" Dan was relieved by the disclosure, but still mystified.

Ed took a large sip of coffee before continuing, "That's too complicated to answer right now, Dan. Just leave it at that for now."

Dan nodded his head, looking downwind. The mound of dirt made by the tractor was easily six feet high. Normally, he would have been bewildered by a supervisor's confession, but he had learned that people liked to confide in him. On the other hand, he was just as frequently shocked by the impression that he was equally mistrusted under certain conditions. The tractor retreated slightly uphill, weaving through the stumps of two trees.

Ed's tone was forthright. "I want you to head the framers, Dan. This job will be a good test for you, I think. What do you think?"

Dan was watching the encroaching smog pattern chalk the sky. "Sure. It shouldn't be a problem. I've been doing this type of work for about two years now."

Ed raised his hand, "Well, you seem to have a knack for it. I'll make you a copy of the architect's floor plan."

"Great. But keep me updated on deadlines, okay?"

Ed's mood finally brightened. "You bet. Hey, that sounds like Pete pulling in. You guys can start before the others, I guess. Hell, the deadline already seems like yesterday...."

A few hours later, along the next ridge, O'Dool targeted the horsefly with a fat palm. His left hand set the tumbler of whiskey onto the deck, while his right positioned over the blot on his right quadriceps. "Touchdown, Rams!" blared from the television, and spurred his attack; but the fly escaped. A telephone ring jolted him upright, and he left the balcony slightly stumbling. He noticed that his wife had left a brassiere on the couch before she flew to her ailing mother in Wisconsin.

"Hello," he fairly barked.

"It's Childs."

"Okay, what do you want?" O'Dool was blunt

"Sorry to call you at home, but Hernandez told me I should call with any information on O'Shea." Child's voice was flat, almost monotonous, and there was a slight, patronizing tone to it, also, which annoyed his fellow officers.

O'Dool dramatically paused. "So what is it, this information? And, by the way, Childs, information is a poor word to use. We look for incriminating evidence in the force."

"Right. Well, Central received a call earlier today. He was causing a disturbance at a dental office." There was an apologetic tone in Childs' voice.

"Was he arrested?"

"Unfortunately, no."

"Was a complaint filed at a precinct house?" O'Dool felt trapped by an encroaching cloud of irrelevance.

"No."

"Then tell me how your information could be called incriminating."

"Well, he was suspected of being under the influence of a narcotic." Childs coughed.

"He was acting erratic?"

Childs was able to recover a bit of his confidence. "He locked himself in a bathroom for at least an hour. He claimed it was from the effects of the Novocain."

"Had he ever had such an adverse reaction to Novocain before? At least according to the dentist?" O'Dool finally felt a slight surge in interest.

"Nothing on file." Childs said it noncommittally.

O'Dool inwardly cursed. "Okay. So he was high, but did you consider that it could have simply been from alcohol, not any illicit substance?" O'Dool sipped his whiskey appreciatively.

"Not exactly. But they said he was acting as if he was under some type of hallucination." Childs' tone was a question unto itself.

"Right. But that could also have been the result of an as yet unreported case of mental illness."

Lengthy pause. O'Dool felt his stomach rumble. He continued, "Look, you never know with a guy like that. For all the time we monitor him, we come up with very little evidence, or what could be even loosely called it. He is always involved in something weird. I don't know…"

"Lieutenant?" Childs sounded a note of desperation.

"Look, let's talk about it more tomorrow. And tell Hernandez to mind his own business. He'll know what I'm talking about."

Childs paused lengthily, and could only lamely reply, "Right."

"Okay. Goodnight."

"Adios."

"Spanish?" O'Dool wondered aloud. "What is going on here?" He considered Hernandez's undue influence. "Adios? What? Is he grooming Childs for a border patrol position down in San Diego?" He shut off the verbal valve, and remanded the chair on the patio. "Maybe Hernandez has a plump mujer cousin for Childs' chubby consumption." He wearily stood up when the phone rang once again.

"Hey, it's Hernandez." Hernandez possessed a cockiness that was somehow likable.

"Now what do you want? Your stooge Childs already called. What are you trying to do? Excite him over nothing?"

"No, chief, we know he excites himself. He doesn't need anyone for that."

"Then why are you getting him worked up over a harmless hippie named O'Shea?" O'Dool's tone was becoming strident.

"Hey, it's the talk of the whole department."

"Already?" O'Dool shook his head and, squatting, pulled down the Venetian blinds.

"Yeah."

"Goddamnit. Now the chief will never let me off this never-ending case. Sometimes I think we're linked because of our common Irish last names."

A lengthy pause. "I doubt it. But I just wanted to call you to let you know that I did not tell Childs to call you tonight…only if he obtained important information."

"Right. Now could I settle in for the evening?" O'Dool swirled the ice cubes in his empty glass.

"Surely." Hernandez suddenly adopted an official tone.

Cheers blared from the television, and he turned to see a Rams receiver spiking the ball in the end zone. "Okay, goodnight, Hernandez."

"Goodnight, jefe."

He kept staring at the phone, expecting another call. His wife Marie was desperate to be with her mother when she died, but also insistent about apprising him of her fluctuating daily health. The contemplation was enough to make him reach for the bottle again, and watch the yellow–and–blue uniforms on the screen become a beacon for his hazy consciousness. Guiltily, he considered calling his brother Pete in Sacramento just to keep the line busy.

Even with the scant light, he could see squirrels cavorting in the trees. It was his favorite Laurel Canyon pastime, accomplished alone, whiskey glass in hand. It soothed him to espy them organizing their own game of hide-and-seek, squashing normal squirrel rivalries. It reminded him of his own competition with Bender before he became chief. Their rivalry had permeated the entire department, and had spilled over to drag racing in the desert. Sometime before the sun had risen in the desert, a young supporter of his had died under mysterious circumstances: Rookie Billy Thompson was coffined in the driver's seat of a Cougar with a broken neck.

In the coastal canyon, the trailer was dark, even in mid-afternoon. It sidled up to a tree-shaded creek, which abutted a short, steep slope that led to the main road. Weeds strangled the struggling patches around the front of the trailer, which had a canopied porch. A trickle of water seeped down slope, toward Billy's territory. The bath drain had been opened about thirty minutes previously, and the two intruders examined the spores of soap scum sinking into the ground. The smaller of the two thumbed a dissipating circle with disgust. "See, I told you they were greasy palefaces."

"Hhmmm." The older one stared, with a blank expression. He was short, stocky, and bearded, with camouflage fatigues that were too baggy, and he practically stumbled in a pair of oversized rubber boots. "You think we should reconnoiter?"

"What is that?" Billy pulled out his Buck knife, and drew circles in the dirt.

"Just what you're carving, boy. We complete a circle around the perimeter first, before we go into a hot spot." The man made a nervous scratching at his own throat with blackened fingernails. His eyes flitted to and fro, looking for intruders.

Billy grimaced. "I guess. I've got to find out if they're hiding more Kid Colt comic books."

The man, named Reed, asked, "You think they're holding out on you?" He crept underneath the trailer and let his hand capture some of the drain. He smeared it into his palms, affecting a clay color.

"What are you doing?" Billy leaned forwards, then backwards.

"Capturing their essence, so they can't smell me." Reed grinned wolfishly, and crept back out.

"Suit yourself. I don't need any help, because I'm not a Paleface." Billy came out the way they had come in, clamping a hand over his mouth. "I think you're talking too loud."

Reed hissed, "No. Charlie won't hear us over the radio. Especially with the static of the canyon."

"Are you sure?" Billy's attention was pricked.

"I think so." Reed craned his head, and stared into the sky. "Absolute blue, we are crazed," he murmured. "Try to make sure you're safe, piss-ant, or you're a dead Marine." Billy's mouth turned down in disgust.

"Stop it. My Mom told me to tell you the war is over."

"War is never over," Reed resumed. "War is a natural outgrowth of people. And, once the physical war ends, the psychological one begins."

Billy's eyes spirited toward a cawing crow, yet he could not, from such a distance, see it arcing in the air. "Mom likes to say stuff like 'destiny does' and 'all pricks die' but I don't know what she means."

Reed nodded. "She probably means that it is all of our destiny to become pricks, since we cannot control destiny." Reed grinned sideways.

Billy hopped forward from behind Reed, then forced himself into a more mature, stately walk. "Hey, don't walk so fast. You'll make animals scared, and then we'll lose our cover."

Reed's voice was hollow. "Everything and everyone retreats from the resolute Marine, because the Marine kills everything in sight."

Billy squinted in the sun, and shielded his face. "Right. But haven't we already reconnoitered?"

"Reconnoitered? I'd say yes." Reed stopped briefly, scanning the sky once more, then continued.

"Well, let's move in again then." Billy turned halfway on his heels, and started a large circle back toward the trailer.

"Okay. You go first, and I'll cover you." Reed pulled out his .357.

"Hey, is that loaded?"

"I'm not sure. Probably." Reed shrugged his wide shoulders.

Billy stopped walking, and began to rip tendons off weed stalks. "Well, I don't know if they deserve to die yet. They're hiding the Kid

Colts, but that's not enough." He reached the first window on the back side of the rusting green trailer, hopping a few times. "Hey, I'm going to need a boost to get in."

"Where's Sara?" Reed sounded fearful for the first time.

"I don't know. Probably in the front reading. My Mom says she is a crazy gypsy Irish woman. The kind that would've got along with our ancestors."

"What kind is that?" Reed was gradually slumping.

Billy waved impatiently. "Stop asking questions, and give me a boost."

"Okay. What do you see?" Reed used his right arm for support, his left only for balance.

"Hold on a minute. It's dark in there. But I don't think anyone's around. It looks like they sleep on the floor. There's a dog sleeping in the corner."

"What kind?" Reed tried to peer in by extending to his toes, but was still too short.

"I don't know. Do you want to ask it? But don't get mad. You've just got to stop asking questions. There are some cowboys and Indians books on the floor right underneath, but I can't tell exactly what they are. They try to make us look evil, not the truly evil palefaces. So I'll have to punish them for that."

Reed spoke in a monotone. "The VC are gluttons for punishment. Put a grenade in their mouths and they don't even flinch. Pour hot oil on them and they still won't talk. But VC women are the toughest. They won't even listen to you when you threaten to rape…"

Billy's legs pushed back slightly. "All right, I get it. Okay? But I see a slingshot on the corner dresser. Maybe we could break in the next time they all leave at the same time. Then I could see if there are any Kid Colt comic books hidden in those cowboys and Indians books."

CHAPTER 5

In a large studio loft space in Venice, the air was thick with smoke. "Fuck, it stinks in here," Harry commented, and rolled over on the couch until his weight rested on his right elbow. From this vantage point, he could more comfortably regard the empty vodka bottles glistening on the low coffee table, basking in the ray of early afternoon light, and the duller t.v. dinner rubbish, a small collection of Tasty Meat Treats and Gourmet Raviolis alongside the remains of deep-buttered eggs.

He lowered his chin to his raised fist for support, and winced. *Goddamn butchers.* "Scrape my gums? What for?" There're barely any teeth to support as it is." He repeated the words aloud as he recalled them, as if applying a salve. "Why don't you just cut out my bloody tongue? Right, Dr. Jeffers?"

"Dr. Zeitgeist won't be returning," he mumbled aloud to himself.

"Christ." There was a sizable slab of meatloaf on the floor, which on initial inspection appeared to be a dropping of human excrement. Eyes pulled away to his cigarette pack, which was flat and burned at the edges. It was as if it had been prematurely made into a makeshift ashtray, a plastic erector set that had miserably failed. "Huh? Another failed design?" he thought. In actuality, he had attempted to flatten it into the shape of a lotus flower, provoked by a t.v. series on horticulture. Cody the leprechaun had banged on his door toward the conclusion, and he had almost employed his shelehleh stick to send a potent message: *Don't interrupt a man in deep contemplation of beauty. Or else be prepared to suffer the sting of a concrete-like wood staff from the Old World.* Grating music from the outside world, along with the spectacle of various flowers, in shutter-like action, opened and spread on the screen. *Purple irises and yellow sunflowers and pink roses.*

"Go away, Cody!"

"You've got to let me in."

"Come back tomorrow!" The banging increased, until Harry's own heart fluttered inside his chest.

He shouted across the space of ten feet toward and through an oak door. "Go away, you fucking weasel!" Finally, Cody departed, but the mood had been destroyed. So Harry turned on the Rockford Files and bemoaned a drug deal gone awry. "Come on, Rockford, give the loser a break."

But the morning had arrived too early, and he expected Cody to return at any time, with enough drug withdrawal energy to kick his door down; like an oversized wet ferret, since he liked to bathe in alley puddles after a dosage of rain.

Harry's hands trembled over the table for purchase of the painkiller bottle, but, instead, encountered a still solvent flask of vodka beneath the ratty tv guide, scalded by a splash of cold coffee. Umpteenth series on upcoming presidential election gracing the cover. He picked it up carefully, and dog-eared that evening's page of listings. "Damn! What happened to Grizzly Adams?" *Mountain Man buried by Charlie's Angels.*

Eventually the medicine was located, and he swallowed the pills with a splash of the vodka, and clicked the silver spaceship remote control. He barely recalled the dental office incident, least of all Bruce. *Benedict Arnold*! "Bruce, I'll get you yet, you fat s.o.b.," he said aloud.

A growling stomach pulled him off the couch. He opened the curved door of the non-defrosting fridge, and pulled out a carton of eggs, and a stick of butter splayed over a tea saucer. He was still wearing the holey Levi's he had worn the previous day, and a long-sleeved plaid shirt which he had not removed for three days. It was spattered with A1 sauce mixed with cigarette ashes.

Cody arrived when he was frying his first egg on the edge of the skillet. It sounded as if he was knocking on the door with a small bowling pin, or even a bowling ball. Harry feared for the integrity of the doorjamb. "Cut it out, Cody! I'm busy!"

"Bullshit!" The raps became more insistent, a booming rat-tat-tat that disturbed the drapery of spider webs hanging from the ceiling. "I need some smack, or…something. Anything!"

"I'm not your sugar daddy. I'm just another poor artist." He could not help but chuckle to himself. "And you're a man not in control of his faculties."

"Yes I am! I'm just tired of you putting me off. Besides, you owe me." The tone of voice had become pitiable, and it was time to flip the eggs, over-easy, wrister style, adding a touch of Tabasco.

Harry was amused. "Putting me off! You're putting me on! You're just a regular scrounger, you wet rag! You ever hear that expression, 'Your story is old?'"

Cody's voice was keening in its self-pity. "I need your help. Okay? Or else my bike will be taken away, it's my only hope, I need something to sell so I can get out of debt, a fucking loan shark is after me, okay?" On the stove, the Tabasco licked flames.

Harry slightly relented. "You're crazy, but if you'll go away for an hour, let me wash up, eat breakfast, dress, I'll try to fix you up with something. Just don't let my eggs go cold. Okay?" His spatula was already poised over the skillet.

"Promise?" The voice was reed thin yet sharp through the front door.

"If I'm still alive, yes, I'll serve you. But go away now." Harry felt it to be a fitting closure.

"I'm gone." Cody flourished one final knock before he left.

Cody returned with a dripping cheeseburger, and ate it quickly, without once uttering a word. He licked the yellow wrapper once for extra juices, then crumpled it. "Okay, Harry. I won't mince my words."

"I hope for your sake you don't, Cody." Harry kept his eyes fixed on Cody's, because he wore an evasive (and almost squeamish) look. "The way you move around my place, looking at things, makes me nervous."

Cody's eyes kept darting, and his thin face was sallow. "Hey, I was just at Bruce's the other week, and he said I made him feel calm..."

"Don't talk back to me about Bruce. He can't be trusted." Harry released a ball of gas, which went unnoticed.

"Well, okay, I don't see what Bruce..." Cody was suddenly exasperated.

"You brought up his name, not me." Harry reveled in the sudden look of disgust on Cody's face.

"Look, Harry, this is my proposition." He picked up a beaded necklace off the floor and weaved it through his fingers.

"Hey, put down those beads. I don't want you putting a spell on me." Harry chuckled.

Cody dropped it, enjoying the brief clacking noise. "Fine. I won't touch anything else. But before I lay this thing out, could I have a valium?"

"All right. Just promise not to ask for another one later today, and tomorrow, and the day after." Harry re-adopted a threatening tone. "You're an incorrigible child."

"Oh, no, Harry. You know I won't do that."

"Okay, we'll refrain from hostilities. Here, catch, Fido." He lofted it through the air.

Cody snatched it like a terrier. "See, you can't throw a pill past me."

"Congratulations then, Fido. Now what's this proposition you're talking about?"

"The bottom line, Harry? A trip down to dirty Tijuana, Mexico."

"No, thanks." Harry folded his arms across his chest.

"But you haven't heard the good part yet." Cody felt adroit in his powers of argument.

"So? Tijuana is like any other border town in the world, full of scumbags, hosebags, douche bags, creeps, geeks, and freaks." Harry suddenly leapt up to extricate his rice paper hanging lamp from a spider web.

"Come on, Harry! Don't you want to play hide the salami with some chica?" Cody grinned wolfishly.

"Yes, but I can do that anytime here with a clean chick." He waved an unlit cigarette at him.

"Like who?" Cody's tone was innocently inquisitive.

"Hey, I'm just saying, I have enough trouble with the crazies of Venice. I don't think I could take more excitement. Besides, what's the plan?" Suddenly, Harry felt unsure.

"I'm still working on it, and I want to surprise you." Cody leaned back in the ripe-smelling couch.

"You s.o.b.. That's what I get for my patience? What kind of business proposition is that?" Harry scowled.

"I just need to work out the details."

"Such as who will fund it? Right? That's the main detail."

"No, you see, I can make a business deal across the border." Cody sounded a note of triumph.

"No, then, because you want me to front you the money. Right?" Harry's ire was rising once more.

"Don't think of it that way. Do you realize how dirt cheap everything is down there? Buy a case of beer, and you redeem the bottles for another half, you know." Cody absently scratched an underarm.

"That's what you've been told, Cody." Harry's tone had a bit of finality to it.

"No, it's what I've seen firsthand with my own taste buds, buddy. And, besides that, there's also great beaches, like Rosarita, that are ridiculously cheap. You just can't go in the water." Cody grimaced.

"Why?"

"Oh, you know, no one goes in. Simple as that. Mexicans think they'll all drown, and we gringos think that we'll get some sort of infection."

"Mexicans shit in the water?" Harry asked in the tone of an anthropological professor.

"Maybe some. But, like I said, most are afraid of the ocean, like it exists with the intent to kill them." Cody felt authoritative on a subject once more.

"Good attitude to have. We can't swim like our reptilian ancestors. We're not rubbery enough, have too many bones." Harry winked.

"I'm telling you it's a can't miss deal. All you have to do is front gas money." Cody adopted his best factual tone.

"And donate my van to the worthy cause?" Harry disgustedly burped.

"Well, that goes without saying. My old Ford is in the shop."

"You mean your leaky garage, asshole. You know, some day you'll learn to speak openly and honestly." Harry's tone was from a great distance.

"I try, Harry." Cody held up his hands in a gesture of supplication.

"Not hard enough." Harry had an urge to spank him with his wood stick, but, instead, went to the freezer and pulled out a fresh bottle of vodka. "You haven't sold me yet, Cody. Not even close. But maybe a drink or two will loosen up your brain congestion."

"Harry, you're a sweet touch, you know that? So here's to drinking together." Cody tapped the rim of his glass between his front teeth.

"What in hell is that?"

"Oh, just something I learned from the secret brotherhood of chipmunks." Cody tittered.

"Go fuck yourself, then. Or maybe put your honkers to use. I've got a chair post here that needs trimming." Harry thwacked it with the stick.

"Are you kidding? I charge over fifty dollars an hour for these buzz saws." Cody was self-impressed.

"Okay, now we're getting somewhere. Let's save the business talk for later." Harry guffawed.

"Sure. We can make a pledge with another shot…or two." Cody was ecstatic.

Harry caressed an itch at the corner of his eye with a knuckle. He gravitated toward the solid chink of the bottle against the glasses as he poured in the limpid light of the room.

CHAPTER 6

O'Dool stared through the latticework of his office window blinds, and felt a pain course through his lower rib region. He took some deep breaths, and was able to reduce the sting to a merely uncomfortable pressure, as green chaff hissed up from the lawnmower growling outside. When the machine approached the window, the green grass formed a brief, floating cloud in front of his window. For an instant, he could apprehend the vision of a yellow bee caught in the haze before furiously buzzing away.

He felt stymied at every turn, and sensed his healthy law enforcement skepticism turning into a molding pessimism. Only when his eyes caught the white bag on the corner of his paper-strewn desk did he recover himself. He was both enthusiastic and pessimistic about Hernandez's constant energy.

Hernandez spotted O'Dool ambling towards him from a distance, and squinted through the light shooting over his shoulder, because O'Dool had not closed his door.

"Hey, chief, why don't you just chain Childs to the fucking desk, ese. Doesn't look like he'll be able to go anywhere for a while."

"Mind your own business, Hernandez." O'Dool thudded past, but dropped a light white bag into his lap on the way to his own desk.

"You drugging me with sugar now, too?"

"Sure am, hombre. I know that you don't drink coffee, but I still thought a fresh brew in your lap might wake you up a bit." O'Dool momentarily halted.

"Hey, why don't you lay off a bit, chief. Just because your wife is upset and…"

"Leave her out of it. She's coming back too soon." O'Dool continued walking.

Hernandez stifled a laugh. "I see."

O'Dool shrugged, and turned back around. "Her mother's a hypochondriac, and a manipulator to boot. She has survived too many supposed terminal illnesses already. Marie's been denying to herself that she's mentally ill for too long."

"Look, chief, Childs and I have an idea."

"Which?"

"Well, we think O'Shea's doctor has him hooked into a sweet prescription pill deal, so he must have some excess to sell."

O'Dool winced, in part because Hernandez had lowered his voice to a loud whisper. "What's new about that? Doctors help patients stay happy?"

"I see what you're saying. It would only be a misdemeanor, but at least it would be a start." Hernandez leaned back in his chair, apparently very self-satisfied.

O'Dool closed the space, and sat on the edge of Hernandez's desk. "Look, cowboy, that will only make him extra cautious. It's better to bide your time, as frustrating as that might be. Or, to put it another way, don't go for the quick fix."

"Hey, Bender told me he wanted results." Hernandez's tone was defiant.

"Screw Bender. He wants something before he retires to cover up for all his past mistakes. Look outside the lines a little bit, Hernandez. Don't you see how he's trying to make you feel big by putting you in charge of Childs? Don't be fooled."

"Okay, but you know that my hunches are usually right, and I have one of those feelings about O'Shea." Hernandez made a slightly strangled sound.

"You're not listening. Whether it's worthy of our time or not, you need to slow down. But why don't we talk about the rest over lunch?" O'Dool stood, and adjusted his belt over his ample girth.

"About when?" Hernandez took a large sip from the coffee cup, and it almost backed up on him.

"Right now. I need to get the rest off my chest before it ruins my day."

Dan swung the hammer four times, and the nail was driven in flush, the second and third strikes the most efficacious. Around him, and in various postures within and on the top of the seams of beams, were groups of twos, measuring, cutting, and nailing. Dan inspected the work as he went, checking for gaps between beams and shoddy nail work. Already, he had studied the lumber for warping, and had sent Murphy and Johnson back to the lumberyard for a small stack of replacements. He made mental notes of the errors as he fixed them, but stopped at individual catalogues, since overall he was pleased with the work. He ignored stony stares, and aspersions to his young supervisor's character (himself).

"Damn," he thought. "This isn't so hard. Much easier than I thought it would be." He did notice a forgotten joint stuck in a lower crevice, and what appeared to be a partial whiskey label detached from a flask, stuck by a sliver of wood, wilting and fading in the sun. His first thought, as he climbed down beams to the edge was, "Finder's keepers," but, upon considering the possible fallout among the crew, desisted. *Is it a good luck charm?* Voices rose to him, like cryptic messages of dimensional wind: "Post, 4X8, joint, 2X4, 26 ¼. Remember, post first, joint second, second and third piles."

Then he was struck with sudden immobility, a pervasive mental condition which sometimes afflicted him in such dosages as to render him a narcolepsy suspect. His balance was slightly compromised, and he put his hand out for support as he stared suspiciously at the crushed joint. He was relieved to notice that no one paid him particular attention, leaving him to awkwardly shift his weight for additional balance. He scratched his two-day stubble absently and whistled, "She'll Be Coming Around the Mountain." It surprised him that his melody did not awaken his worker bees, as he imagined them buzzing in a harmony. *Only a nearby squirrel would deign to answer their call.*

It could not have lasted more than one minute, but by the time he had reclaimed his consciousness, he felt dilatory. He scurried to find overlooked details of work, and popped a stick of gum in to work his rusting jaw, even tapping some beams merely to hear the sound of his effort.

"Hey, Dan?"

"Yeah."

"You mind if we go to lunch a little early? We want to check the early race results." He cracked some knuckles by clenching a fist.

"Yeah. Go ahead. Just make sure you're back in an hour." Dan was a bit unsure, and unsteady.

"You don't have to tell us that, Dan." He already had his work belt out, and the sound of it striking a makeshift wood pile rattled Dan. *"Damn," he thought, "these guys can be loud. Fast, though. Maybe too fast."* His wiry body carried him down to the ground, where the bright silver catering truck had already materialized, struggling up from the smoggy valley.

"Jose?" Jose had a short, scraggly beard, and an aversion to small talk.

"Yeah, it's me, amigo."

"Give me the usual. But extra sugar. I'm sluggish today."

Hernandez's left pinkie had been skewered early in the morning, when he had stooped to pick up his newspaper, as if even the cacti in his yard were prone to punish those who recounted past events. Hernandez was inclined to feel that keeping abreast of current events gave him a more secure footing in law enforcement circles. But the stinging pain did not prevent him from tapping his desk while thumbing through the files with his left hand. To his thinking, O'Shea's innocence only existed on the surface, and he was determined to crack the code. He left the jacket of his new, brown polyester suit draped over his chair to signal his desk was busy, then dawdled over another file until O'Dool was ready to depart.

Hernandez held his hand up. O'Dool had the stem of a green pepper between his thumb and forefinger, raising it to eye level. A young Mexican girl sitting behind Hernandez giggled at the display, and flapped the arms of her Barbie doll. Beyond her, a mariachi band in black sequins and sombreros played a variation of "Mi Amor" with the aroma of frijoles parading through the space.

"What's wrong?" O'Dool asked.

"I don't think you know what you're doing, amigo." There was only a scant tone of questioning in Hernandez's voice.

"Sure I do. I know a jalapeno when I see one." O'Dool bit half off, chewed once, then scrambled to bring the glass of water to his lips. Hernandez's mouth twitched at the corners. O'Dool drank the entire glass, and slammed it down, a bead of sweat already forming on his forehead. "Fuck, what was that?"

"That was a green jalapeno pepper." Hernandez contained his mirth.

"Bullshit, Hernandez. I've been to Maria's many times, and I've had jalapenos. That was something different."

"No, amigo. There are two types of jalapenos." Hernandez winked at the snickering girl.

"Don't fuck with me." O'Dool was pleading.

"No, really, amigo." Hernandez paused to quickly dip a chip in the red salsa, throw it in his mouth, and dismantle it. "There are two green jalapenos. One is lighter, smaller, and more shrunken looking. It is the sweet one. The other, as you already know, is hot, dark, and juicier."

"So why didn't you tell me?" O'Dool's tone was injured.

"I tried, but, as usual, you were too stubborn to listen." Hernandez leaned back in his chair and admired a waitress filing past.

O'Dool was warming to the mariachi band, one of his feet doing a quick gyration on the tile adobe floor. "Well, it doesn't make sense. You say the smaller one is sweet, but why is the light red pepper as hot as hell?"

"It's a red pepper, not a green one, and it's dark, not light, it's like comparing, how do you gringos like to say it..." Hernandez held his chin.

"An apple and an orange?" O'Dool was disgusted.

"Exactly." Hernandez's palm started tapping on the top of the table.

"Bullshit," O'Dool blurted. "An apple is a different kind of fruit than an orange. But a pepper is a pepper."

"Then why does one pepper put your mouth on fire and another not?" Hernandez leaned back with his arms widened in an expansive gesture.

"Because people who are supposed to tell you don't." O'Dool was only beginning to warm up.

"Sure, blame me again for not knowing. Don't be so sure, and maybe I'll buy you some cervezas." Hernandez was drawing him out slowly.

"How generous of you. I guess that means I'm supposed to buy the food?" O'Dool's voice was flat.

"Well, honestly, amigo, that was what I was hoping…Wah,wah, wah," he sang along to the Spanish horn.

"Forget it, and your amigo talk. I've got enough trouble paying for my wife's vacation expenses as it is." O'Dool practically spat it out.

"I could tell you which foods are spicier?" Hernandez winked.

"No. I'll just stay away from peppers. Maybe I'll stick to the bean and cheese burrito. Yeah, that's what I'll do."

"Well, here comes our waiter." The middle-aged man was graying at the temples, but his face was free of lines. "Senor, my amigo would like one bean –and- cheese burrito, and I'll have the enchiladas de pollo."

"Anything to drink, senores?"

"We'll have two Dos Equis," O'Dool said. "Some lime on the side, too, please."

"Certainly. I'll have the cervezas for you in no time." The waiter gave a slight bow before turning on his heels.

"This is the best restaurant in Boyle Heights, amigo. You probably noticed how polite our waiter was. Well, the owner, Luis Ortega, hires only professionals, who might have just come from Mexico. They don't last that long here, because they usually find work in schools or clinics. Some locals think they're too elite here, but the customers don't complain."

"I can't." The waiter returned, and poured half of each beer in a chilled glass and placed a small dish of limes between them. "But let's talk about how our chief is bending your ear." O'Dool had regained his ground.

"Very funny. Now I know you have a sick sense of humor, like me." Hernandez held up a five dollar bill toward the mariachis, signaling them to continue.

"Don't sidestep the issue, Hernandez." O'Dool drank off half the glass in one gulp. "He did the same thing to me early in my career, pulling my chain."

"And it worked out pretty well for you, right?" Hernandez snickered.

"Let me finish. He pulled my chain, and I advanced at Rampart, his turf. Okay? But he's known to not like seeing his rookies leave the nest. Why? Because that way he can more easily protect his reputation."

"But where would you want to go, anyway?" Hernandez asked.

O'Dool shrugged. "I don't know. I've always liked the desert, maybe a city like Phoenix, but more likely an old Western town like Tombstone." O'Dool looked off into the distance toward the front door.

"You into that cowboys and Indians shit?" Hernandez was clearly amused.

"A little. But getting back to my point, if I was you I wouldn't get too involved with Bender and his cronies. It might seem good now, but when you get to my age, you'll regret it."

Hernandez drank quickly. "I see your point, but Bender will be retiring pretty soon. He has to. I mean, isn't he in his early sixties already?"

O'Dool was unmoved. "Doesn't matter. Either way, you'll be hooked into his network. They'll still call him at home while he finishes off his fifth vodka-and-tonic. Even when he's basically dead, he'll still pull some strings at Rampart."

"You know, he says that if I do well on this O'Shea case..." Hernandez leaned forward.

"Shit, there is no 'O'Shea' case to speak of. At least not yet. He hasn't made one false move yet. He's either the slipperiest guy on the planet, or the most innocent." He waved over a busboy. "Two more cervezas, please. I figure, Hernandez, that he is not much more fucked up than me, or anyone else, for that matter." O'Dool smiled, as if pleased by his own tone.

"Nah. That guy's a doped-up loser. No real contact with a family, and no woman on his arm that we can establish." The younger cop sounded certain.

O'Dool's tone was factual. "You really do believe all the crap Bender is feeding you. You're too young for your own good. When you get to my age you won't be so judgmental."

Hernandez clapped his palm atop the table once more. "Look, I try to keep it as simple as possible. Isn't that what cops are supposed to do?"

"That's the general idea. But I think a cop has to back off of vendettas. We're not in the business of harassing people." O'Dool stopped himself in mid-sentence.

Hernandez grinned wolfishly. "Yeah, tell that to some of my homies around here, or the brothers down in Watts."

O'Dool reset his shoulders. "You know what I'm getting at, Hernandez. I'm worried that if you stick with this O'Shea business, you'll start seeing things, and I don't just mean real things, just so you can get the case moving."

"Whatever you say, amigo, but I'm already locked in. Bender won't let me back out from here." Hernandez tried to inject a tone of finality.

"You should have talked to me before. You could be in for a lot of trouble. But here comes our food. Let's try to get another subject going, or I don't think I'll be able to enjoy eating. Tell me a little about your family."

O'Dool thought that Hernandez would not divulge much, and he was correct.

Sara felt that their lives were successfully incomplete; a mysterious work in progress within her young boys and her husband Dan's characteristically humble yet frenzied stabs at a mystery through symbolic attempts to grasp the invisible; aided by the rusting blue trailer's land, an Indian-on-peyote's dream landscape, beyond the brutal glare of the sprawling city beneath them, lodged in endless lights. Her own poetry reflecting the irony that the fullness of their mostly barren land made them ancient tenants, or, on the other hand, simply brief but appreciative caretakers.

She lit a cigarette, and gazed into the virtually pitch black sky, here and there shot through with purple vestiges of the sunset.

Sara stuck a divining finger into the pot of water heating on the stove, reflexively pulling it out after a few seconds, and came into more direct focus in the glare of candlelight.

"Mom, water's cold in here." Big brother's voice was quivering yet confident.

"Already?"

"Yeah. Make sure the next pot is really hot. Okay?" He splashed around for punctuation.

"Okay, I have a good batch here." She smiled at her selection of words, because she was never very fond of concocting cookie batches, or other pantry food dessert types. She had one last dreg of her cigarette, then stubbed it out in the ashtray. She shoved aside the Indian blanket curtain, that had a feathered serpent on the inside (bathroom) side, and smiled at her older son. "Now, put your feet up, because it might be a shock at first."

"I can take it." However, his voice was glum.

"Don't argue with me. I'm trying my best." Sara almost failed in sounding stern.

"Okay. I guess it could hurt." He winced with imagination.

"Well, I know it would, so don't start trouble with me, honey." She playfully tugged at one of the splashing feet, and poured the contents of the pot beneath them.

"Mom, Billy and Weirdo have been spying on us." His tone was playfully insistent.

"First, honey, you shouldn't call that man 'Weirdo.' His name is Reid. He was sent to a war, and he probably saw bad things."

"Then why didn't he leave?" He leaned forward.

"He was in the military, honey, where you have to do what your bosses tell you to do." She felt there was not much more for her to say.

"So that's where he learned to spy?" His voice was gradually growing louder.

She smiled. "I guess you could say that. They make you do all kinds of things in the military."

"Like kill people."

"Unfortunately, yes." Sara was surprised by her lack of indecision, but then she figured her boy already knew.

"I would never kill anyone, even if someone told me to, except for maybe that creep Weirdo." He slapped the water between his knees.

"Sean! Don't talk like that. Perish the thought. You're letting him get too much to you. Billy, too. I'm going to have a talk with his mother."

"Please don't do that, Mom. He'll know, and then he'll really think we're wusses." His tone was suddenly self-pitying.

"I'm sorry, but I'm your mother, and I care too much about you to let you be harassed like this." She handed him a bar of soap.

"It's okay, Mom. Really. I hate Weirdo, and I kind of wish he would just go away, but I'm not mean like him." He stared at the small soap bubbles.

"That sounds better, honey, but I still don't like that you called him 'Weirdo' again. Besides, you must like him somehow or else you would never talk to him."

"Yeah, but I've never actually talked to him, and Billy has never told me." He stared past her to the stove with a questioning expression.

"Okay. So ask him next time you see him. Everyone deserves a name." She reached for a plaid towel in preparation, and laid it on the storage chest.

"You mean Billy?" He sounded shocked.

"Of course Billy. But now let me get another pot of hot water so you can rinse off." Her movements were quick but unhurried.

CHAPTER 7

Dan laid the joint aside in his Venice studio, and fell onto the sofa, grinning ear-to-ear, relieved to be away from the construction site, which was beginning to feel strangely unnatural. A stretched canvass leaned against the far brick wall, empty except for a barely described (penciled) circle. He watched it slowly emerge, a line becoming suddenly squiggly. *A brazen snake. It detached from the circle, and squirmed across the snow field. It bled onto the borders, and leapt off.*

Serpentine shapes serenaded the air. Visions of Sara trapped in the trailer cleaved the liquid composition. Fire arrows and tomahawks raining from the sky. Cochise hair ablaze.

Pot crackled in the glass jar rising like ignited sawdust. Embers adrift, rising to the bare ceiling. Images of decapitated Custer and frozen Plains warriors. Blood cresting the privy hole. Snakes red in human waste. Sara running to the nearest store.

He covered his eyes, but did not hide. Eyelashes twirled in the pupil. Red cavalry sabers cross the forehead. Canvass collects sharp incisions. Now a frozen circle.

After an hour of rearranging reality, he pushed himself up to drive home to the canyon.

A few miles away, stasis shoved Cody to the ground. He had attempted to rise from the chair with a fifth of whiskey clutched in each hand. He twisted to land on his back and preserved his scant backside, staring at the sky through the skylight.

"You fool! You think I would've let you escape with my treasure?" Harry menacingly hovered.

"Stop! You hairy monster!" Cody set the bottles back on the table between them, and sat back down, favoring his left buttock.

"Harry monster? I have long hair and a beard, but, believe me, I'm far from hairy overall. But I could show you the one hair on my dick."

"Shut up. I think you're hurting from Jenny girl." Cody struggled back to the couch.

"Jenny girl moved to Frisco, I think. She told me I wasn't hip enough anymore." Harry wiped an imaginary tear from his eye.

"Screw her, then. She never gave me a chance, and I'm less of a burnout case than you are."

"I beg to differ, Cody. Who else but you is stupid enough to admit liking 'Leave It to Beaver'?"

"I don't care, man. It's a great show. A gal like Jen would never understand it. But I don't care either way." He stared at a psychology textbook smothered by the dust from Harry's book shelf.

"No, you care too much about women. It's better for them to care about you." Harry chuckled.

"What are you talking about?" Cody's eyes detached from the case.

"A woman wants to take care of her man, that's what. That's what every woman wants."

"You're scaring me, man. What have you been doing lately, putting your nose in psychology books?" He pointedly stared at the crusted shelf once more.

"Yeah, among other things. I've probably sniffed too much resin lately." Harry thought he saw a black widow skidding off the spine of The Female Animal, a thickset volume directly below the psychology book.

"Whatever it is…"

"Yeah, right. You want some of it." Harry maneuvered into a sleeping position on the couch and gazed through the skylight at the gray sky, encumbered by fog. "I hate the fog. I would rather it snow."

"It doesn't snow in L.A. You need to go to the mountains." Cody appeared perturbed by the necessity to explain.

"You didn't have to tell me that. If it is not sunny, it might as well snow," Harry declared, leaning back.

"Whatever, Harry. You have only weather forecasts for me?" Cody spoke under his breath, as if suddenly hesitant to speak.

"Not exactly. But the future doesn't bode well for us, you know." Harry was unsuccessful in raising an eyebrow.

"Speak for yourself." Cody snapped.

"Drink your whiskey, and let me finish. The future doesn't bode well for us, because, oh, fuck, you get the idea." Harry's hand shot out to slap the air.

"Not exactly. Why don't you finish?" Cody leaned forward.

"Okay, asshole. Artists such as ourselves are doomed to create order out of chaos, which is the most difficult thing one could ever attempt to do."

"No, the most difficult thing is finding a decent broad." Cody's tone was facetiously authoritative.

"Suit yourself. The reason you don't get any action is that you stress yourself too much. You need to put yourself in the right situation, and then just let things flow." Harry smiled at his own explanation.

"Yeah, you're right. Like Tijuana. You go down there, and the women are just waiting for you." Cody grinned.

"That's right, for me, not you," Harry dissented.

"Screw you. If you had more women around, you wouldn't be popping pills and drinking all day and night." Cody jerked to his feet momentarily, then sat back down.

"So now you're the expert on women, huh? Are you keeping track of your many encounters?" Harry did not leaven his sarcasm.

"Not exactly. But maybe I'll start in Tijuana." Cody was defiant.

"I see where this is headed again." Harry thought that Cody's imagined encounters could fill a dossier.

"Imagine, Harry. Sweet girls that you can fondle and plant all night for a meager sum." His obvious reference to gardening, one of Harry's pursuits, did some discredit to him.

"You practiced this routine at home, right? Harry was momentarily triumphant.

Cody stood and declared, "Tequila and beer flowing all night, amigo! Bright light bulbs in the clubs, not that Las Vegas neon shit. A real natural light show!"

Harry deadpanned, "You know, Cody, somewhere a dog farted when you said that."

Dan had jostled the kids, mussing their hair and tickling them while Sara crowed behind them, folding their superhero pajamas recently hung out to dry; watching the purple candle drip into a ceramic elephant holder. A large grasshopper clicked against the window screen while the boys struggled to loosen their father's grip.

An hour later, Dan felt nimble and malicious. His hands gripped the handle of the hoe, waiting for the proper moment to strike. He had been pursuing his enemy, the one who had threatened his family, by blocking the route to the privy for nearly ten minutes. The dirty skin crawled over the ground toward the trailer, rustling the bushes, a stalker who had frightened Sara and the kids. Momentarily, he considered giving the instigator a warning, but his head was still throbbing from the block of wood that almost cleaved his left temple when it shot off the router, adding to his impatience and discomfort.

Light spangled the ground around the transient, and he quickly raised the hoe and struck downward with his summoned strength. The force paralyzed the body, and the large head was half-severed. Blood had yet to flow from the mouth when he leaned down and, putting his entire weight behind his right palm, bluntly shoved the hoe through the rest of the neck tissue. He did not turn the body over to examine the face, instead appreciating the adrenaline of the kill.

However, nausea followed quickly, and he realized that he had not killed another breathing organism since he was a child. But what right did the transient have to exist? Almost reflexively, he kicked the head away from the still squirming body and said, "Should we eat you for dinner? Breaded rattlesnake is quite delicious." His pronunciation lingered on the last word.

When O'Dool felt pressed, he tended to frequent construction sites, since humming activity tended to calm his own thoughts. He was beset by the thought that his wife and career had hijacked him, leaving him with only desperate stabs at serenity.

O'Dool carefully trimmed the overhanging cheese slice from the white bread and balled it up, while ahead of his dirty windshield a wrecking ball demolished the remains of an old brick warehouse. The last letter of the once proud business name of Spergman was briefly juxtaposed with the "O" of the wrecking ball to accost O'Dool in the negative as he raised the salaciously-soggy mayonnaise sandwich to jaw line. NO. A corner of it detached itself and fell onto his right loafer while the dust from the proximate dirt cloud settled. "Hhmmm." He picked the morsel off his shoe top and quickly dispatched it without further ado.

Within a half hour, he was seated back at his station desk, flipping through unsolved homicide case photos, biding his time before his meeting with Chief Bender. Absently, he pulled some paperclips loose, re-stocking his desk stash. He espied Childs leafing through the O'Shea file again, careful to leave the red index flap face down, despite the fact that the sheer weight of it beggared description. "Eat it up, frankfurter boy," he thought. He flipped the photos nonchalantly, since they were of the common type, not the grisly crime scene variety. Still, some of the young faces gave him pause. Images of the newly minted dead stared at him in black-and-white glossy finish, like 1940s era chorus girls.

One of the young faces made him flip back, and he had a strong urge to demand quiet from Childs, who was giggling over some minutes of the O'Shea file. Even as he engrossed himself, he was curious, wondering why he had never recognized the face in the past. Did Hernandez have Childs float some in as a joke? He flipped the print over to verify its source: Diana Carrillo. Dark, petite features, except for a protuberant nose. Simple, low-cut blouse; Billy Thomson's (deceased rookie cop) girl, who he had paraded at police picnics. She was the victim of a vehicular accident involving alcohol, and O'Dool wondered if there was any connection. Billy just a sweet simpleton caught in the folds of cop intrigue. "Should have protected him better, but, bastard that I am..." He imagined Jones leveling him with a reproving look. "But what does he know anyway?" he thought, reaching for a can of Tab. Bender had Lieutenant Smith make sure he comfortably edged into retirement with the least amount of regrets and complaints under the strained circumstances. Everyone knew that Mayor Enfield was blistering the department, favoring Jones over Bender or O'Dool himself, even though his advancing age sparked tremors of humor during the morning briefings. "Hey, how much have you been getting of the old love, Jones?"

As for Fitzsimmons, well, he was uncanny about solving crimes, and had the best rapport of anyone in the entire Rampart division, but his loathing of paperwork had always weighed against him. And his prolific and enduring bachelorhood plagued his image in the conservative trends of the department, which attempted to squash as many "titty bar rumors" as was feasible under the lecherous conditions. O'Dool himself was not entirely immune to the contagion. He replaced the photo, but set it off at an angle for future inspection.

Childs had a fit of flatulence, a true bugler's call, interrupted by a coterie of cops in their finest garb, badges shining, cutting through the desks like huge spangled flags, or pimps of enforcement.

O'Dool watched their backs recede, kneading his sore right knuckle. "New rookie brass?" he thought. "Why are they here?" He watched Childs, a recent rookie himself, sneer at their military stride.

He urged his right index finger into the barrel of a gun, and exhaled in a voice loud enough for O'Dool to hear, "Whoosh!"

O'Dool, despite himself, smiled and shook his head in sympathy.

The last of the indoctrinated recruits paused and turned, his hairy, stubby arms wide at his sides, as if fighting to maintain balance.

O'Dool wondered if he had caught Childs' defecatory scent, or, on the other hand, if he had merely sensed the derision.

Childs buried his nose back into a file, and the moment passed without incident.

O'Dool had that pleasurable feeling which accompanies solitary rest. He even propped his feet onto his desk and sunk further back into his chair, regarding the meeting preliminaries with a bemused and long-winded yawn. He nodded with encouragement when Detective Fitzsimmons strode through, resplendent in his white bucks and wavy, greased coif, fingering his Hawaiian tie. O'Dool pulled an old handkerchief out, and placed it over his ruddy face and daydreamed while the coffee cart sped past.

Harry blurrily sighted the collapsed chair, which Cody had crushed while attempting to leap to the exposed ceiling beam. But the mode of total recall eluded him. All he could retain was the ferret-like being promising a spectacular exit: "I'm the egg man."

"No, you're the walrus." Harry raised his fist like a sledgehammer.

"Fuck you, I'm the egg man." Cody's voice was nasal.

"O.k., then I'll crush your head into egg yolk." Harry rocked his fist in the air.

Had he actually pounced onto his friend like a panther, thereby effecting the destruction of the chair? Or had he simply spurred Cody into a preemptive action? Did he elude Harry, poised to strike with his claws (unclipped fingernails)? He espied a few greasy strands of Cody's prematurely gray-flecked hair on the crumb-infested floor, and the torn remains of a Zippo papers packet. His head screeched, "Reach for the aspirin bottle," but he picked up the remains of a beer instead.

CHAPTER 8

C hief Bender, as was his wont, tapped the ledger pad with a pencil while he speeded the proceedings: "Fitz, sit, O'Dool, welcome, Childs, o.k., Hernandez, patience, patience, Smith, how's it going today? While you get settled I have to forewarn you all that the county commissioner's office could be sending an auditor out at any time, so let's try to be on our best behavior."

"Fitz chimed in, "I try, I try, I try try try try try try, I can't get no..."

"Enough, Fitz. The party's over. No young women here, except for you tittering girls" (Fitz finished the lyrics under his breath, and punched O'Dool on the arm). O'Dool himself noticed that a picture of Bender fishing in the Florida Keys had found its way among the Wall of Distinction in old block English lettering, proclaiming, "Hail to the man who rises above the fray," which he concluded was a poor and liberal paraphrase of a famous poet. Further, he detected a flash of disdain on one of Bender's fellow anglers, as if the fish hook had almost lodged into his chubby face with an erratic cast of Bender's red-white-and blue striped rod.

"Man the torpedoes, gentlemen."

Bender snapped: "I said that's enough, Fitz. I've got out-of-town brass coming in for the rest of the day, so I need to get things going quickly."

A few murmurs of assent, and many grumbles, ensued, while O'Dool secreted two tootsie rolls like chaws of tobacco inside his shave-chapped cheek.

"But the first order of business is to get some volunteers for firearms training. Our chief instructors have to deal with over recruitment this year, so there's not enough ballistics people on hand. We have to get people slated within a couple of weeks."

Smith seconded, "You'll be up for medals of commendation and seniority for departmental openings. You can expect a personal recommendation from myself in the bargain, also."

Bender resumed: "But let's not rush it, guys. There's no need for everyone to volunteer at once. Unless you guys all choose to decline just to make me look bad." He exchanged a chuckle with Smith, who sat directly opposite him at the end of the long conference table. But no ripples of hilarity followed, which almost made Fitzsimmons choke on a tootsie roll in a chasm of delight.

"Of course, if I get no volunteers whatsoever, I will not hesitate to assign a few of you officers."

"Now, moving on to other matters, I have word that the East Side Locos are planning a raid against the Boyle Heights Lobos. Friday night, Hernandez, I want you bandanna in hand (Hernandez appreciably colored in agitation) and Childs, I want you as outside observer. Both of you guys will create a diversion in event of some conflict erupting. No, Fitz, you're not going to Spanish lessons on company time, so stop looking at me like that. And, O'Dool, don't take the night off. I want you to start working overtime on the O'Shea case, but I"ll brief you on that later, after the meeting, one-on-one. For the time being, I want input on a number of matters. I've created an employee suggestion form, so I'll leave you all in privacy for about twenty minutes while I have more coffee brought in" (exit to applause).

Fitz was not hesitant. "O.k., guys, here's the scoop. You pay me, and I promise to take a spot."

O'Dool was not humored. "Sure, and I'll just wear the pope's nose. How about if I just take one position now, and save you all the trouble?"

"That would still leave one," Fitz interjected. "You all realize he'll want to chafe one of you rookies, right? Unless Childs forfeits as he should."

"What?"

"You heard me, Childs. You never were a straight shooter, you know."

Hernandez chuckled. "Now what do you mean by that, hombre?"

"It means he spills his seed" (Smith exited the room, frowning).

"No, hombre, it means he's a traitor," Hernandez retorted.

"Right, to Oscar Mayer frankfurters," O'Dool could not help but add.

"Right on, Childs, way to plug on." Fitzsimmons had a distinctive cackling laugh that made his lower lip tremble.

Childs controlled his voice. "You know, Fitz, you should be named Child, the way you act. I'm surprised…"

"Ohhh!" (the reaction was decidedly underwhelming).

Childs was unfazed. "Really, you're just a grown, spoiled brat. Or what my English mother would properly call boorish" (round of applause).

"Bravo, chubby boy. You hit the nail on the head, didn't you?"

"Maybe we should actually discuss what we're supposed to?" O'Dool remonstrated. "You guys are sick."

"Speak for yourself, O'Dool. I see that wink in your eye all the time, I can even see it now."

"You're drunk, or halfway to it," O'Dool said in a monotone.

"You're right. But, then, I'm in my element." Fitzsimmons relaxed.

"How so?" Childs pursued. "You're stirring up trouble, just pretending to care about something."

"Hey, guys, when did he become my mother?" (slaps on backs brushed past ears). Fitzsimmons support was still strong with the backbenchers.

"When his mother slapped you both." O'Dool leaned back, and let the laughter cleave the air. Smith's re-entrance did not subdue the mood.

"All right, guys, I see you haven't been productively discussing the chief's point while I've been gone. So let's dig in now, or I'll start making my own suggestions to him." Smith's hands tightened around the speaker lectern.

"Alright, I suggest we take a vote on who is going to volunteer to be shot by young eager cadets." Childs raised his hand.

"It's not live rounds, you idiot, Childs. We're not as foolish as you." Smith chuckled, but it was far from a generous gesture. His narrow face crunched up into a scowl. "You'd be wise to stop your horseshit, and that goes for all of you. I keep telling the chief you all act like little girls when he's not around."

"And what do we act like when you're around?" O'Dool, with his ample seniority, could afford to continue prodding him. "Are we just little boys then?"

Smith abruptly pulled a gun from the small of his back, and placed in on the middle of the table. "I'm going to spin it, and whoever it hits will have a chance to volunteer to the chief when he returns. Yeah, I know what you're thinking-'That's not what he said', but I don't care. None of you are straight shooters anyway." When he spun the Smith & Wesson, O'Dool saw the intensity of his look. "And do me a favor, try to write something of value on the suggestion form."

Sara threw the tomato can beyond the porch, and sighed. Archie, the smallest of the three mongrel dogs, had cornered the catch, snarling at his competitors. His tongue flicked into the cylinder, gnashing his teeth in fury. His appetite, concentrated in his rasping tongue, was unappeasable, and he even caught Sara in its vortex. She reasoned that he would only continue to rage if not fed to the point of exhaustion. Even the crows seemed to circle far overhead.

She picked at the ground meat container, and started forming meatballs. Of course, Archie continued to snarl incessantly, while the other two larger dogs genuflected and whimpered, buffeted by an unnaturally strong ocean breeze current.

It swirled the sprig of hair on the camouflaged warrior's head (Reed), bundled with first aid gauze arm bands against the prickly weeds. His eyes scoured the upward terrain for rattlesnake tunnels, and his ears pricked for a dog patrol. His thin lips were sun-blistered, and his right ankle throbbed from tripping over his moonshine bottle secreted in Billy's mother's garden shed. However, he could not recall the intervening two to three morning hours, in which he and Billy had quarreled again over stalking tactics.

Sara heard some rustling outdoors, and fought an urge to scream discontent out the slatted window. The kids were safely ensconced in their respective school classrooms, and she pictured them resilient after falls to the black playground mats, which made her think of Billy and the grizzled veteran. "Animals were once men," she thought, and made an abortive move away from the stove, toward the small writing desk in the corner, which was piled high with grant proposal pamphlets. Wind flicked the edge of "Natural Arts Institute" with the faint indentation of a coffee cup (slight gray on a field of gold). She ventured that Archie was even stirring up varmints. The clicking of his tongue was unarguably sending the surrounding ants into a frenzy.

Reed, the crouching warrior, lowered the day pack from his shoulders and unzipped the small compartment to pull out a peanut butter and jelly sandwich that was neatly cut into four slices. "Day rations," he thought, and eschewed the water canteen for the time being. He and Billy had discussed the comic book crimes over a bowl of muskrat. Or, rather, was it simply a bowl of Wheaties or Raisin Bran? He did not particularly approve of the way Billy ordered him to put two spoonfuls each into the red plastic bowls that usually contained what Billy termed "mother's drippings," pork doused in green chili, as if she had a talent for Mexican concoctions to begin with. She traded inferior recipes for Sara's sumptuous pasta dishes, filtering Winston cigarette smoke through the pans on the crusty stove. Even the normally immune warrior's taste buds were bothered by the contradictory cooking currents.

Thus, the warrior's nose was inexorably drawn toward the low slung green trailer with the slow drain and comic book heroes.

The meeting at Rampart continued. Bender presided over the fluorescent-lighted and linoleum-floored room. "O.k., Smith. Tell me who is going into ballistics." Coffee in Styrofoam cups lined both edges of the table, and dried sugar solidified on the polished surface.

"Listen, I need to take care of this issue as soon as possible, because there are other matters to discuss."

"It's Fitz and Hernandez for the time being, chief. I'll have their signatures before the end of the day." Fitz and Hernandez exchanged the "thumbs up" two rows apart.

Bender coughed. "Good. Now, let's move on. Friday is the number one priority. Hernandez, you're really Johnny-on-the-spot. So I want you to start calling for backup."

"But, chief," Hernandez had an aggressive streak, which Bender admired despite himself.

"No arguments. You've seen the file on the Locos and Lobos, so you know that the summer action is heating up. I want the whole department on alert. We'll set up headquarters in the Sears parking lot. Everyone in this room will be briefed there, and we'll have patrol cars at our disposal. Now, let's not overlook safety. I want all of your weapons checked through ballistics, and your autos run through the shop. Smith here will coordinate the times tomorrow and Thursday. And let's call it a short one, men. I need a chance to put up my feet up between this meeting and the next…"

"O'Dool, follow me to my office." Bender did not wait for a response. Instead, he inferred a stubborn refusal, the kind which could lead to another whiskey shot after work (for them both, but apart, of course). "Don't malinger by the coffee machine now. Treat this as a foretaste of the next meeting in the event you still treat this as a joke. In that case, I'll have to chew you out in front of your colleagues." His right index finger tapped on the top of the cubicle walls like a miniature sledgehammer. "You seem to distrust my gut feeling about O'Shea, which irks me, almost to distraction, as a matter of fact." Here he paused to reflect on an empty Styrofoam cup leaning askance, wedged into the space between the bottom of the wall and the white Formica floor. He made a preemptive move toward it, his right arm temporarily like a large minute hand, then ratcheted it back, favoring his shoulder. "Don't upset this old man, O'Dool. Damn it, there's no one around, and I know you like to decline a seat when I take you into my office. You know, this O'Shea case can't leave me with my pants down?"

O'Dool took a deep breath. "The Feds are mistaken on this one, chief. I've got a gut feeling about it. This guy's just a washed-out hippie. Couldn't be much of a dealer or a supplier, as far as I see it."

Bender's right hand clamped to the top of the partition wall. "Well, there's the problem. I've got a suspicion that you've got a soft spot for this hippie, it's just that I can't quite figure out why."

O'Dool shrugged. "Nothing, chief, besides the fact he's being put under unjust surveillance."

"Who said he's under surveillance? If you've been spreading rumors about a dragnet you'd be wise to rest." Bender's face was red.

"Okay. But then you think the Feds have anything on him?" O'Dool pressed the point.

"I don't know. But if they ever take over jurisdiction, my department can't be made to look as if it's been playing with its pants down. So don't worry about O'Shea. Do your job, and you might learn something." Bender did not deign to wait for a reply. His gait was straight and long and his chin jutted out as he advanced down the hallway.

Harry drove somnolently, burdened with the weight of whiskey sorrow: "What rapacious barkeep emptied my wallet?" The 101 freeway between Sunset Blvd. and the Harbor interchange was an unsettling blur, riddled with decaying jalopies with busted, milky white tail lights, and an occasional red-white-and-blue speeding police cruiser. "Calamity changes course," he thought, as he jerked back and forth, exit lane to slow lane. A stab in his gut made him wince, but he could not recollect the offender. "Better me than him." "What!" he expectorated onto the dashboard. His challenged motor skills were making the act of shifting gears somewhat problematic, and he punched the offending knob more than once in frustration. He imagined being pulled over and responding with a smart reply: "Sir, my barkeep contributed to the delinquency of a drunkard."

He espied the shimmering Bonaventure Hotel through a blurry left eye, and almost clipped the back bumper of a Mercedes. "Oh, cheri amour!" (he preferred the bumps of reflectors to the smooth transitions of painted lines).

But then he saw a man spidering up the shimmering walls. "What am I seeing? Who has come to visit," he said aloud. He watched the elevator ascend to the top, muttering to himself about solitary, aspiring men of all cloths, "Philosophers the worse, death to all schema!…where do we go from here?" Again, another isolated recollection of the bar, a raised knife and the shining of the Hell's

Angels wings on the wide leather jacket, and a backpedaling slickster in a brown suit.

He caught a fleeting glimpse of an overabundant afro hugging the roof of a black Mercedes speeding down the freeway. Entranced by the red taillights, he almost missed the interchange, fumbling for control. He was worried that he might miss Chalmers' performance piece, which he assumed would entail the destruction of assorted car parts with gigantic power tools.

Chalmers never appeared. Harry cursed his infamous name to anyone who would listen-"A marionette, he is!" gathered on the Bel Air lawn in various poses of unconcern. One woman had ventured into the darkened flora, and returned with a cactus glare: "Fuck. I've never seen such as that. Must be genetically engineered! No way they could grow irises prettier than mine."

Chalmers had been there at some juncture, however. There was an innocuous flower pot beside a sledgehammer with a rose sticker on the blade. "Don't you all understand?" Harry spluttered. "He thinks he's fooled us with an installation piece!"

"Hey, chill and smoke some dope."

"Yeah, you need to calm down."

"Right on. Pippen here has the gas."

"The gas? I'll show you some gas. I'm going to drive my bus through his fucking front door." Harry was verging on a complete breakdown.

"No, really, he pulls this routine once in a while. You shouldn't take it personally."

"I shouldn't? Why not?" Harry's tone was actually plaintive, as if he truly wanted to be agreeable.

"Because we can have our own party." Pippen smoothed his hair. "I've got just the right mix…"

"Yeah, and Tricky Dick here has some moonshine, direct from Mexico."

"Right. And Lucy here will pick you some flowers."

Harry was not entirely enamored of a flower picking arrangement, but he assented anyway. Pippen courted the crowd. "Now, this little party is on me. But don't forget to take my number down before you leave, so you'll never be short on supply. Or just give Chalmers a buzz." Harry forced himself to socialize a bit, in order to be regarded as kin to the crowd, but he was too anxious to accede to the request of picking his own flower arrangement. He excused himself after perhaps an hour, and proceeded directly home. His body slightly swayed, but the marijuana had gently mastered his mind.

CHAPTER 9

O'Dool watched the rain bead on the living room window, sipping a whiskey-and-water (he had neglected to check his soda supply in the morning). Then the water streaked to the floor grooves of the deck, spurting down slope with various spigots. O'Dool stared past the television and adroitly slipped off his day loafers, willing himself to relax. Marie would be returning within the week, and he already pictured her proudly irritable, complaining about her mother.

He clicked the television remote, and, seemingly without purpose, sped through sitcoms, looking at the squiggly screen through the distorted lens of his cocktail glass. His bent was toward the fetishes of tawdry sex and gratuitous violence which he normally reproved.

He grimaced as he thought of his dispute with Bender. His lingering suspicion was that he would increasingly be demonized by the chief and his dupes. He realized that once a person was labeled a questioner, a decision was quickly reached that he was dispensable; no, even that he had to be discarded.

"Fear is laid to rest with this glass," he softly reminded himself, and consumed the remaining contents in one constricted gulp. Then he effected a forced settlement of the hovering question, fixing on Charlie's Angels. It was the kind of flippant foreground noise that he required, just the right amount of levity subtracting from his potent malady. He was upright and reached for a cocktail napkin and utilized it as a sketch pad. His caricatures of police brass had drawn the ire of incoming and outgoing devotees, but the response, in the form of unofficial complaints, had not moved him. In fact, the deceased Billy Thompson himself had compelled his illustrative critiques due to his penchant for wearing plaid pants every day of the week. It did not help matters that Billy's ever-changing girlfriends color-coordinated themselves with his poor taste.

O'Dool would goad Thompson into admission that his fashion statement was the extent of his surrender to conformity. But O'Dool could sense a great deal of resentment about Thompson's so-called "charisma," one that (so whispers imputed to him) would make him a potential departmental enemy.

O'Dool could not completely disregard some complicity in the fatal chain, in the sense that he had never warned Billy to be cautious; and seeing the deceased girlfriend's photo at such a recent date made him particularly suspicious of police malfeasance.

O'Dool watched the rain pour diagonally across the deck, directed by the gusting wind. He wondered how much additional wetness the already deteriorating boards could sustain, since he had been neglecting to reseal them for years. He clutched the glass to his chest. Methods of change in a torrid August-a certain confrontation with his wife, Bender's intransigence, and a querulous stomach-did not deter him from drinking. He pictured his squirrel friends imbibing in the torrent, almost as recklessly as him.

Through his magnified sights, Reed hallucinated, and the blue trailer quivered like a giant mound of gelatin. He adjusted the binoculars from his elbows. He wondered, "A rabbit hutch? Or an infant Jesus' crib?" Weed burrs nestled in his cotton fatigues. A tickle of sweat dribbled down his muscular flanks. His eyes adjusted to the soft sunset inching toward the comic book heroes' lair, hovering like a giant, pink saucer. He unsheathed his Bowie knife and notched a small wood dowel produced from his pocket. *To remind himself. One click.*

He surmised he could locate Charlie from cooking smells wafting downwind. But what exactly was that shape? It behooved him to adjust the glasses. But he still could not be sure. Maybe Billy was playing another prank on him. But, regardless, he could sense the danger. He disregarded the mysterious shape and focused on obtaining another click through the weed vines. He proceeded with a swiping stick to forewarn any rattlers. Could not, as yet, see Sara reading on the porch. He began to think that the shape was a hallucination. He finally disregarded it and proceeded more hastily.

Porkchops and onions. Unmistakable. He wetted his lips and tried to imagine a side dish. "Cucumbers succulating in oil?" he wondered. Then he detected the wholesome scent of baked potatoes. *Charlie must be returning soon to his base.* He gouged the ground with his knife and aggrieved a retreating lizard. Spurred him to uncover nearby rocks in search of pursuers. The lizard paused, but did not turn its head. "Eyes in the back of his head," Reed thought. *A skull like an arrowhead.* Burst to nearest cover when he raised the knife. "Billy Boy," he muttered to himself. "Billy Boy come out. Over." But his cohort was clearly hiding. He guessed behind the outhouse. His nose keened with the pork chop scent, drawing him forward, and he decided to reconnoiter via the privy.

Sara heard a rustling. Realized it was her boys wrestling. An argument had started over possession of a Kid Colt comic book. Quickly degenerated into a scuffle only lacking in hair pulling and Indian burns. Sara puzzled over a Shakespeare soliloquy in a pocket paperback nestled in her hands. "Words too ripe for infertile minds," she mused. "But I refuse to be a helpless squaw woman." She turned the meat sizzling on the stove and waited for the wails of the defeated little brother to alert her. But she felt slightly inactive. She proposed that she could still act beyond a mere "damsel in distress." *Perhaps evocative of a fiery Jane Russell caught in a canyon drama: "Chase rattlesnakes with a rake," she thought.*

Dan was late. He had called earlier to tell her he was keen on another pre-dinner studio session. He was frustrated because his boss,

Ed, had again moved up the construction deadline. He had left the construction site with a hunger for whimsical shapes (and Pinks chili dogs).

When the chops were brown at the edges, she flipped them, and added a dash of pepper. General rustling noises reached her from the romper room. She poured water to boil for the macaroni-and-cheese from the bathtub faucet into a metal bucket. The sloshing reminded her of her younger son's first bath. He had protested that he would be sucked down the drain.

There was a long shadow at the end of the porch when the water came to a boil. She noted that it possessed appendages, even as it crawled away in the glare of her flashlight. When she mixed the butter and milk with the cheese mix, she sensed that there was another shadow in the vicinity. But when her older boy rushed in and grabbed her leg, she barely flinched.

The truck had stalled. Dan pulled the choke but the engine would not turn over. He pumped the clutch. "Shit. I just rebuilt the bastard." Engine coughing, as if in urgency that even a machine is not the same after surgery. Caught on Bundy Drive near Santa Monica Boulevard. On a street with new, bright pastel cookie-cutter cottages, direct from Candyland. "Sure. Try to soften the desert landscape," he thought. "Why didn't you just fill the streets with palm trees and broken-down ice cream trucks?" The quicker he pulled the choke, the less apt the engine was to start. He felt the unwarranted stares of the suspicious, accusing him of potential theft.

He considered the plastic monolith as he opened the hood and began to grapple with the loose ignition wires. "Ultimate presumption? Or wise assimilation?" But which of the coiled wires were not grounded (indecision plagued the day)? He went to the truck bed to retrieve his tool box. He fended off wires with pliers. How would he weave different colors into resin? What is it that Ed had told him earlier, about there being two ways: the fast way and the right way? (No doubt he was referring to the construction deadline).

He disentangled the jumper cables and, in hooking them up, drew a spark from the two arms. He replaced them and went back to the cab to turn the key, press the gas, and pull the choke. He took care to keep the battery acid and grease away from his Levi's. "How many did I ruin as a teenager from rubbing oil into the denim?" Pulled a red rag from underneath the seat to wipe his hands. He espied two kids on bikes circling him from across the street. One pointed a plastic bat at his chest and cackled with a mouthful of purple candy. He waved back, not quite as amused. He extended the peace sign when the engine turned over, but the two bicyclists had already turned the corner.

Harry stood bowlegged over the toilet bowl, or, at least, so he thought. When a particularly harsh hangover visited him, he had to struggle for equilibrium, and consequently tended to walk with his legs further apart (whether this would actually constitute a bowlegged gait is up for debate). His urine escaped in small spurts, and his legs faintly twitched. Even though he scrupulously avoided it, he still caught a bit of his reflection in the bathroom mirror. The uncomfortable condition did not behoove him to reflect long on his preparations for the later-in-the-day jaunt to Tijuana. Cody was intent on driving straight through, but Harry had a hankering for a late afternoon siesta in San Diego. Or, perhaps, even a shrimp cocktail in Long Beach with enough horseradish to burn through his pain. "Hell," he thought, "I can get back in bed, because I've got nothing to pack." One raggedy pair of Levi's, sneakers, and one freshly laundered tee-shirt would do. It would also be more feasible to purchase a drug stash in San Diego. "This weasel Cody will have a connection," he thought. "Once you let him in your door, you can't get rid of him. Hell, even the broads pity him for some reason."

The drug issue made him think of that time they tired to outrun the cops in a jalopy station wagon. When a delivery truck had impeded their progress, they had screeched to a stop, and a can of resin had exploded from the back seat.

Their heads were like glazed donuts, but the material covering their heads was thick, and painfully sweet, burning like sugar. Harry had collected himself as best as he could, choking off his own giggles, concentrating on a palm tree beyond the police cruiser, waving in the wind.

"Excuse me, officer, could you call the fire department. My head feels like it's on fire."

"Sir, I do not like the looks of your vehicle." The young officer, with neatly shaved sideburns below the official police hat, grimaced.

"Well, officer, I agree it is a bit on the clunky side, but it does get one around." Harry pressed his right elbow against Cody's floating rib, because he sensed an outburst.

The cop shook his head and grimaced once more. "Right." The agitated shuffle of the cop's feet was like crackling popcorn on the concrete. His shocked look was hidden behind dark sunglasses.

Harry adopted an official tone, and lowered his voice one octave. "But, officer, I think you should back away. My buddy and I are used to the fumes, but they might knock you out."

"Right." The cop absently waved in front of his face, and turned back toward the patrol car, slightly swaying. "What a couple of freaks," he said to his partner, who was cradling a shotgun. Meanwhile, Harry and Cody frantically wiped their heads with old newspapers, which only served to make them look like papier mache dolls.

An approximation of their conversation:

"Hey, give me some of those lingerie ads."

"Screw you. I told you to make sure the drum was sealed."

"No, you didn't. Besides, you didn't have to slam on the brakes."

"You faulting my impeccable driving now? Why don't you just stick your head back between that broad's legs?"

"Why? Because I can tell you've already been there."

"Forget it. Just fish that water gallon from behind the seat. Then empty it on our heads."

In the neighborhoods of East L.A. and Reseda, respectively, the two cops prepared for their undercover assignment on a blistering day:

Its colors were black-and-red, in proper checkerboard pattern. Hernandez set the razor down and wrapped the scarf around his head, the last of the shavings trickling down the slow drain. It comforted his aftershave-stung scalp. Wrapped in perfect thirds, it covered his eyebrows and rested on the thin bridge of his nose. He leveled his gaze at the mirror, and blinked from the fumes: "Si, hombre. Vamos, cholo," he said to his reflection.

Childs reached into the cereal box, and cursed. "Damn. The treat is always at the bottom." Despite his slow, purposeful digging technique, the overspill of sugary treats dispersed across the table. With one hand, he swept them singly into the other palm and, his belly, suddenly freed from his damp bathrobe, smeared the edge of the table with the sweat of his exertions and osmosis from the spilled bottle of aftershave. "I'm a cereal psycho," he said.

When Dan arrived, Sara noticed the brief, bright shimmer of light flooding through the boys' back room window, reaching the floor transept of the kitchen and living room. Halfway down the snaking drive, the lights then took a peek at the Mondrian poster pegged into the faux wood wall, and furnished the brown furniture with a cream tint.

Simmering in a pot, the stew could not quite cover the steady scent of the dry dog food remains. "They're counting on some savory leftovers," she thought. Corn bread was already cooling, and the apple pie was losing its lift. Boys in the back sleeping off a virus. Steadily snug in pajamas and leeching mentholadum, secure in two days' rest, until Monday morning. There was scant chance of raising them for dinner without a row.

There was a cadence of barks toward the still idling engine, the competitive energy source. Quick leaps from padded feet, shadows across the light beams. *Propitious for sniper fire.*

Rolling Stones blared from the radio. Engine dead, lights out. The lean man exited reaching for a gray cowboy hat, scratching a face partially clad by a beard.

But then there was a trundle of softer feet behind her. A lone cat that never slept alone pawed the air around her bare ankles. Molly her name. Harry unaffectionately called her "Puss." She heard an unaccompanied stir from the boys' room. Like a locust. Signal of what?

"Smells good, honey." Dan embraced her as the dogs struggled to squeeze through the cracked screen door. "Damn. Hey, guys, enough. Can't you see we're busy?"

"You look tired, honey." She rubbed her palm across his forehead, like a divining tool.

Dan spoke in a flat tone. "Yeah. Ed is running us ragged. He acts as if he'll be fired if we don't finish in record time."

"How is the crew reacting?" Sara rummaged in the kitchen drawer for napkins.

"Too sure of themselves. They act as if they know something I don't. That's what worries me. They almost work harder than I can push them."

Sara adopted a defiant tone. "Well, that's a luxury. What do you think they'd do if you told them to take it easy?"

"Haven't really thought of that." He re-latched the screen door, and smiled at Archie's bared teeth. "You'd keep them in line, wouldn't you, little guy?" He waved his hand in the air and Archie playfully snarled.

"He wouldn't be good for worker morale, honey." She pecked his cheek, and, reconsidered, for the time, the stalker tale.

Dan qualified, "He snaps at everything. But let's sit down and eat." He extricated his large key set from his pocket and threw it onto the couch, which obligingly bounced it to the edge. "By the way, we need to invite Harry over for dinner sometime. You know, have him bring his new girlfriend."

"Who is that?" Sara raised an eyebrow.

"I don't know yet." Dan deadpanned.

"Very funny. I think you goad him into some of his foolishness."

Dan appeared hurt. "Not true. You can't believe that."

"Yes, I can. You're one of the people that puts him on a stage. He feels he can't fail under any circumstances. He has to entertain at all costs."

Dan's voiced lifted. "Don't all artists? I mean, I have to justify us living in a trailer. Otherwise, we'd simply be poor white trash, right?"

Sara cut the discussion short. "No, because we are well read, and have open minds. Let's not get into hypotheticals."

Dan sat. "Okay. But what do you think would happen if I tried to balance this whole piece of corn bread on my fork?"

Sara turned back toward the stove and said, "I think you'd miss out on dessert."

Harry fumbled through the kitchen drawer, rudely pushing aside hard plastic Barbie Dolls and miniature rubber King Kongs. He separated a Big Bird specimen from its embrace with a supine Pokey, turned, and aimed it beak-first at Cody's groin. It caught the edge of the chair, and the head duly snapped off, rolling back toward Harry's feet.

"Hey, quit it, Harry." Cody's voice was clearly drugged.

"Shut up, asshole," Harry snapped.

Cody struggled out of a slouching position in the couch. "What are you looking for anyway? If I'm right about what I'm thinking, you need to find better places to stash..."

"No, this is a true toy stash. It's just that sometimes I store other needed weaponry here." Harry, now on all fours, had his bony ass on display.

"Like?" Cody half-stood, then sat back down.

"Like never mind. You'll soon find out," Harry lobbed over his shoulder.

"Hey, man, why do you have to treat me like this? I'm not a kid, you know, and..." Cody half-stood again.

"Quiet! I think I've finally found what I need." Harry stood, with his back turned. "I promised you that I would enlighten you." Turning, he revealed the two needles held between thumb and pinkie.

"So what's your point?" He gestured with his bottle of beer. "Are you Twinkle Bell or something?"

Harry shrugged. "No. I'm going to prick your ears, so you can really tune into my wisdom."

"What do you mean?" Cody's eyes shot toward the door.

"I mean, I think I should permanently prick your ears into the side of your head." Harry said it in his best clinical, doctor's tone.

"What for?" Cody's voice was a bit panicked.

"So you can be as smart as the vulcan Spock," Harry declared.

"Just stay away from me with those needles." Cody spat out the statement like a curse.

"Hey, little boy, I only want to darn your socks."

"Get away from me, maniac! Hey! You promised we'd leave after finishing our beers." Cody began to move in earnest this time.

Harry recused himself. "I did? Damn, I did, didn't I? Well, finish that off, then, and we'll fly out of here."

Harry struggled to free his left side from the embrace of the door. He held a sleeping bag under his left arm, along with an old, bent fishing pool, and a moth-eaten one volume encyclopedia. If he had been able to, he would have reached over with his right hand and removed at least one item from the bulky mix, but it was preoccupied with a two-foot Madonna statue and a thick Mexican sleeping blanket. Cody had walked around the corner for a beer cooler restocking and snack purchase, so his extraction went by excruciating inches. If Harry had thought of it in such terms, he would have imagined dissolving a solitary tooth to gain release. "I shouldn't go," he thought. "Would be better to stay home. Feed on the carcasses of pigs."

The VW bus was just beyond his reach, sliding door open. Once he freed his hands, he planned to heave the belongings directly inside. But it was then that he noticed a sizable oil slick puddling at his feet. "Damn Carlos," he thought. "Always changes his oil at my front door." Pondering a proper mode of revenge, the encyclopedia slipped from his grasp, and he grimaced as he heard the crunch of the binding.

"Hey!" Harry felt a soft impact on his shoulder, then heard the dull clank of metal on concrete. Reflexively, he dropped the rest of his belongings and spun on his heels, crouched for an attack. He focused on his assailant, but was able to register the Budweiser insignia on the can, the drunkard's afterthought.

Cody was cackling, and cutting a ragged jig. "There, you fat, bearded fuck."

"Okay. That's it. We're not going."

"No, Harry, you can't."

"Yes, I can, so you had better help me pick up the rest of this shit."

Cody made the back tires spin in the oil before the tread could properly catch, and Harry was thrown back in the seat, because he was rifling through the glove compartment, through the stash of ketchup packets, straws, and napkins, for purchase of a matchbook. He suffered a minor case of whiplash.

"Damn, you're in a hurry!"

Cody ground the gears, finally shifting into second. He sang, "'We've got to get out of this place, if it's the last thing we ever do.'"

CHAPTER 10

O'Dool had received the call while staring at the mildewing green shower tiles. He realized that his wife Marie would castigate him for his dereliction of cleaning duties, while he adjusted the shower head into massage mode. He did not particularly rush, taking care to wipe the steam from the slowly cracking mirror. When he picked up the phone to be told that he had to attend an urgent meeting on his day off in the Wilshire district, he held the receiver away so he could curse in the direction of Marie's brightly colored Weebles Wobbles collection atop the kitchen counter.

O'Dool's thoughts wavered in the stuffy office conference room among FBI agents.

"Bend her over. Federal agent tough to get her eye. Chief deigns to include me. Flyswatter hands mimic authority. Cooling coffee bitter sans sugar. Watch her lithe legs. Libido on another bender. Sun spangles Federal Building. Century City no shade. Eyes burn for no chance to protect them. Would have to salute table (inimical to presiding Chief Bender)."

Bender had his arms folded over his ample girth, which had popped out a button of his white dress shirt over his navel. "Okay, O'Dool. What is your input?"

O'Dool nodded at the female agent. "What's my directive?" He had snoozed through the fifteen minute preamble.

She smirked, and tapped her monogrammed pen on top of her clasped leather notebook. Her lips wore the bubblegum lipstick color that O'Dool admired. "Please refresh him, chief."

Bender jutted forward. "O'Dool, I hope you've been following us."

O'Dool's eyes followed the reflected rays of sunlight. "Have I? Yes. Following every, alright. How often do I have to report?"

Bender frowned. "You report anything of substance, or whenever an agent contacts you. What else is there?"

The female agent resumed, "We truly appreciate the opportunity to work with you, Officer O'Dool."

Older Baldy ball-buster (her partner), said, "And we thank you in advance for your cooperation."

O'Dool thought, "Sure. I thank you for the most hypocritical conversation ever to grace the stuffy confines of this L.A. police plaza, I thank you most of all for the smooth, creamy legs of a young female agent, footed by vamp pumps. I thank you for the generosity of a corpulent, gassy windbag boss, and the beneficences of their most hallowed FBI (Fried Brains Incorporated). I thank you for the return of my perpetual complainer wife, and, most of all, with the knowledge that this glorious meeting will soon emblazon the notebook of Chief Bender as a distant memory."

Bender: "O'Shea is en route to Tijuana, and you'll be following him."

O'Dool quickly reawakened. "But that's out of our jurisdiction…"

Bender scoffed, and winked at the female agent. "Don't worry about that. The agents here have taken pains to clear it with all the authorities involved. They are using this as a case study in how effectively local law enforcement can respond to a federal emergency."

Bender thought, "Right. In other words, you want to wash your hands of the shit. Instead, he said, "Excellent. But how am I supposed to tail him down there?"

Female agent resumed: "You'll be flown to San Diego in a few hours. There you'll meet another agent fluent in Spanish."

Bender barged in: "These agents were generous enough to make allowances for a bilingual agent as, otherwise, you would've had to get a crash course on the plane."

O'Dool thought, "Apt choice of words, ignoramus," but instead said, "What kind?"

Baldy cracked: "Well, it's a type of twin prop. You shouldn't be concerned about the actual make, because the FBI only employs the most superior equipment." O'Dool thought, "Did they imprint the company blueprint on your brain? Lobotomize your intellect?" Instead, he said, "Right."

Baldy resumed, "You will also be accompanied by our resident filmmaker. We hope to use footage of the events in the near future at our training headquarters in Quantico."

Female agent smirked. "But, by all means, Officer O'Dool, do not feel self-conscious. We are striving for the utmost authenticity…"

Chief chuckled. "No watered down version, all right? Just don't drink your interpreter under the table. He's a bit of a lightweight, from what I hear."

Baldy busted up: "Ha, ha! And Mexicans think all of us gringos are lightweights!"

O'Dool returned to his reverie. "By all means, Baldy ball-buster, speak your racist mind. By all means, don't mop up the wad of spit you expectorated from your verbal vein. Piss our your remaining vinegar."

Female agent smirked. "You are not empowered to arrest the suspect, under any circumstances. Agent Vallejo will be consulting us constantly on developments, and will make a determination himself."

Baldy: "But, O'Dool, we are relying on you for critical and reliable evidence."

"Sure," he thought. "Cut off my balls before you send me into a brothel. Could I opt for early retirement instead? Why don't you just revoke my privilege to live?" He said, "What kind of evidence?"

Female agent smirked. "What kind? You have been disposed to be more acquainted with the particulars of the O'Shea file. Therefore, we will in many cases defer to your judgment."

Bender resumed, "But don't let the adulation go to your head. We need you to be vigilant at all times."

O'Dool thought, "Scriptwriters? What speech should I make? *Caffeine-hydrated brain fizzled.* How to frame proper words in the stilted lexicon of FBI (For Boring Individuals)? Perhaps challenge the female agent to a naked fireside joust of Scrabble." O'Dool gulped down the rest of the cold coffee. "At any rate, I'm ready to go."

Hernandez confiscated Childs' morning paper, inspected it briefly, and removed the sports page. Replaced it in the general vicinity where it once rested, next to an ice plant bush still drying from a recent watering, in its soggy foundation dirt. Still humming a partial melody of a song he could not recover entirely intact from sleep. He sensed suspicious neighborhood eyes cast on his bandanna-bedecked head, his baggy chinos and black corduroy slippers. "Si, I'm here to cut your pinche perro's (dog's) throat." He critiqued the lawn and found it in keeping with the sloppy cop. Dogshit droppings and overgrown weeds. Shards of bright discarded plastic toys. Eyesore of an entire neighborhood, the constipated cop.

Childs purchased toilet paper in bulk. He struggled with the thought that it might aid his ailing digestion. *Power of persuasion.* He slumped with a cool hand towel draped over his head. Authentic walnut toilet seat requiring new coat of stain pricked his buttocks while he kneaded a ball of toilet paper into dough.

He started with the banging door, and fumbled with his loose sweatpants. He recovered balance with an awkward elbow thrust to the wall, and cursed with the thud. "Hold on, damn it!" He almost slipped to the ground undercut by yesterday's slick sports page. Then he detected the smell of burning coffee. "It's early, so what's the rush?" As usual, he peeked through the front curtain to confirm his suspicion.

"Quit whining, chubby, and open the door." Hernandez threw the Lobos gang sign.

Dan cracked open the 7-Up can, and returned the belated salute of Aaron passing in his Waggoneer. Aaron was prone to complain of stomach cramps late in the afternoon, and hobble on his gimpy leg and groan with each lift. Dan, tradition-bound, sent them off every Friday, hailed in return by longnecks and tallboys. Jerry flourished adieu with a dirt lot, dust-raising donut that choked tailpipes and seized sinuses.

Engine crouched, idling. Trees barely moved by the breeze. As if slightly electrified. Ed en route for a word. Progress report. "Well, to be honest, Ed, I've never seen a crew work so fast without any prodding. Almost disconcerting." *Bonus, boys?*

"Where is Harry? Phone just rings. Perhaps he flew back east. To petition for a further piece of his family nest egg? Maybe he scurried to Vegas for a gambling bender. *One scuttling crab drawn to water.* On the other hand, might simply be in one of his funks. Minding his cactus plants?"

Ed's brow was wet. Slicked it with a palm. Lowered the radio volume, and measured his breath. "One, no damn, two, bastards on my back," he thought. "Bigger than monkeys. Apes. Jockeying for position as I steer through the curves." Bicyclists clogged the too narrow road. "Too late to turn back." He subdued the impulse to sheer off an overhanging mailbox. *Shatter it into kindling for winter warmth, and stuff rich pot-bellied stoves.*

He settled in behind Dan and secured two beading Bud cans in paper bags too long. Rolled up the excess at the tops. Rubbed the water droplets through the diluted wood until smooth, then slapped the dangling key chain. Once. Twice. "Shut up and drink your beer," he thought.

Dan cracked down the loose rattling window, offered his hand. Crowned by the brown can. He blinked in the sun. "Thanks, Ed."

Ed smiled. "Sure. Hey, you deserve it. The guys have been busting their asses…"

"Well?"

Ed shifted in place. "Okay. You've got me. They've been working hard." He slathered his face from hairline to chin. "They always work for you."

Dan thought, "I guess I have a way without words," then said, "Hey, I'll work for a Bud any day."

"You don't say. It's a beautiful day to be up here in the canyon, shooting the shit. Isn't it?" Ed did, indeed, relax in the rare afternoon breeze.

"Sure is. Not quite as pretty as my canyon, though. Can't smell the salt of the sea up here."

Ed leaned against the slightly rusting cab, and manipulated some pops from his can. "I'd like to save money and build a house up here some day. You know, one of those huge deals on stilts, country-style." He flashed a tight grin.

"Well, I guess you've got the crew to finish it in record time. Don't you?"

"I guess. These jobs aren't as fun as they used to be, though. I'm getting old fast, I guess." Ed waved at an over flying hawk, in a vain attempt to purchase its soul.

Silence. "Ed, you know I've got no complaints. I feel I've got a great crew..."

Ed raised his can. "And two angels and a beautiful wife at home..."

"Yeah...more than I probably deserve..."

Ed's voice became clearer. "Hey, no false modesty here. I had my chances when I was younger, and I blew it. Now I'm stuck with unseemly politics...but forget about that."

"What?" Dan felt he was close to an admission of some sort.

"Never mind, I'll tell you in due time." Cast his eye toward the construction site. Noted dust clouds. A West Coast version of Mafia law-"sleeps with unseemly politics"-sprang from Ed's mind, to rest with the fallen leaves.

Close to the edge little brother stood. He was waving the sprig of a branch like a wand high above the heads of big brother and Billy wrestling at the side of the drive like wildcats in vortex. Big brother's bright yellow-and-blue jacket subduing Billy's navy blue sweater. Vortex slowed and the sunlight seeped into his back, diving over the roadway hill. He threw a small rock at them, but the echo was underwhelming. Barely twitched a slight branch as stone tears a leaf.

Billy swore, and the words temporarily laced big brother, struggling to free himself from a tenacious grasp. Fists to the stomach. Once. Twice. Grip unbroken. "Let him go, Billy! I'm getting bored." He jumped for emphasis.

"Screw you! I can still beat him." Billy spit viciously, but the flak descended back to his own cheeks.

"Say 'uncle' and I'll let you go."

Little brother pondered a dash down the hill, but the weeds were too prickly and thick for admittance. He heaved a handful of pebbles, but none struck their intended target. Instead, they spattered the driveway. "Quit it! We called a truce!" He hopped on each isolated foot and U.S. Cavalry code seeped into his speech: "Cease and desist....dumb galoots!"

Billy was still under big brother, flecked by his own spittle. He was praying for serpent fire to singe the Paleface. Big brother was triumphant: "Call me Long Knife!" he shouted.

Reed, the edgy Marine in the bushes, was just out of sight. He counted the rolls of the combatants, and chewed a plug of chewing tobacco, spitting in a 1:2 ratio. Two emptied sardine tins succoring Swiss Army knife rested beside him. He discerned a sheen of oil on the blade. He raised it to lick it clean, then pointed the tip of the knife at the boys, to goad them to further action.

Little brother stood close to the brink, fired by the sun and momentary ascendancy. His raised arm was the divining rod to affect a pleasing closure. No blood drawn.

Billy sputtered, and Big brother pinned his arms. Reed slapped his own face with the knife in the bushes. *Charlie's wiry arms difficult to resist. Sticky jungle vines.* Little brother created his own Sundance. Pirouetted deftly in the air, and landed like a setting eagle.

Then scents of grilled cheese assaulted their noses. Like smoke signals. Little brother remained on the slight rise, warmed by the sun to his core, but nipped on the skin by a sprightly ocean breeze current. "Quit it! Lunchtime, guys!" he shouted. Finally, he disregarded danger, and bolted down the hill.

Cody's shifting technique became erratic near San Clemente. At first, Harry thought he was transfixed by a convertible VW filled with bikinied girls. Gradually, though, he came to attribute it to post-alcohol-intoxication nerves. His eyes had a virtual desiccated look, and his long, bony fingers spastically tapped the steering wheel. "Hey, let's stop."

"Yeah? Why?" Cody was stubborn.

"It looks like you need a drink, and I know I need one." Harry's hands were sweating.

"Where?"

Harry exploded, "I don't know! Just pull off the fucking road."

"Maybe if you stop cursing I will."

"Okay, shrinking violet, whatever you say. I'm not going to argue with you. Hey, maybe I should call you Bruce Junior." Harry's eyes fastened on the freeway divider wall, a generic brick network being constructed off the right shoulder.

"Leave him out of it. You need to lay off a little, you know? Stop frothing at the mouth all the time." Cody changed lanes abruptly.

"'Frothing at the mouth,' huh? You been reading your Dick Tracy comic books again?"

"Screw you. Can't you see I'm trying to move over to the exit? Or would you rather we crash?" Cody sounded as if he welcomed such a disaster.

"Don't threaten me with disaster. I'll tell you when to crash. Until then, don't drive like a fucking mangled corpse." Harry giggled.

"Hey, I thought I was a skeleton. When did I become a?" Cody quickly changed lanes.

"Just drive. And take a right up there at the brick warehouse. There must be a dingy bar around here somewhere. Perhaps a Hell's Angels den." To Harry's eyes, the area was comfortably commercial in appearance.

"Don't count on it. Remember, you're in Orange County now." Cody's voice sounded a note of disgust.

"Yeah, people who hate L.A. because they can't afford it. They'd live in garages…"

"What?"

"Never mind, just keep an eye on the road. I'll scope out our libation possibilities."

"What about liberation?" Cody sounded self-satisfied.

Harry still stared at the orange-vested freeway crew, as if they were a spreading virus. "Never mind. Just turn right at the next corner. Wherever there are hookers, a watering hole can't be far behind."

"I haven't seen any whores yet." Cody's eyes flitted from corner to corner.

Harry briefly sampled an English accent. "Neither have I for certain. But some tend to hide their…"

"Okay, you can stop jerking off. Maybe you'll find one in a bar…" Cody sped up.

"Who said I want to lower my standards?" Harry was smiling again.

"Stop, all right? Just calm down. You're making me nervous."

"Sorry. This is taking too long. We'll just stop at the next liquor store, and figure out the bar business from there."

"'We'll?' Watch who you speak for. I'm driving here." Cody pumped the brakes for emphasis.

Harry's eyes finally latched on. "Look. There's a liquor sign on that grimy window. If it's not a store, it must be a bar."

Cody ground into neutral, and pumped the barely responsive brakes. "I think we need some more brake fluid, Harry." The engine coughed, as the bus shadowed a Blue Ford Fairmont coupe shorn of hubcaps. "Maybe a new engine would do the trick?"

"Look, asshole. You're along for the ride. You're lucky I let you convince me to take this trip. Or else about now you'd be trying to sink your teeth into some fat ass."

Cody shoved into reverse. "You're full of shit. You want this road trip as bad as me. Anyway, you couldn't stop our momentum if you tried."

"Stop saying 'we,' all right? I'm you, and..." Harry was temporarily flustered.

"You don't have to finish. You're getting repetitive, man." Cody spat it out.

"You mean you want to pull the needle off my broken record?" Harry's tone was deranged.

"Right," Cody stated.

"Okay. Just don't scratch my brain when you do it."

Cody turned the key and exhaled deeply. His red-rimmed eyes were moist. He read the fading plastic window sticker: Smith's Liquors. "You're a cruel bastard," he stated.

"Huh?" Harry was briefly taken aback.

"Hey, here's some of your own medicine: 'With that winnowy beard you must be a filthy oral sex artist."

"Now you're offending me, and every woman I ever slept with. Besides, you don't know what 'winnowy' means. What movie did you steal that line from?"

"Fuck off."

But Harry was already on the sidewalk, pulling his holey Levi's up over his bony ass. Unbeknownst to the counter help, he stenciled his initials into the dust-coated glass with a moist thumb: HPO. "Health Provider Open?" he thought. "Anyone for martinis?"

CHAPTER 11

In the car, Childs cleared his throat and adjusted his bandanna and snuck out a touch of flatulence. The odor sank harmlessly into the blue plastic seat. He dabbed at the greasy hairstyling goop at the edges of his sideburns, and turned purposely to the driver. "Hey, ese. What's up, holmes?"

Hernandez grimaced. "Don't even try that again. You sound like a clown. No, I take that back. You are a clown."

"Well, I could still paint my face with lipstick." Childs patted his own bulging waistline.

Hernandez pressed the accelerator for emphasis. "Remember, you don't have to say a word. I'm going to do all the talking."

Childs noted the encroaching traffic ahead, which was typical heading east in L.A., like an endless array of army ants foraging for the downtown queen. "Don't I even have a name?"

"Don't worry about that. I'll figure that out if I need to introduce you. Probably 'El Gordo' would do." Hernandez shot past a trailer truck on the right, almost kissing the safety rail.

"What does that mean?" Childs attempted to not sound insulted.

"It means 'the fat one,' all right?"

"No one messes with a fat man, right? I thought you had more imagination than that." Childs waved at a young woman in her convertible Fiat, who abruptly turned her face away from him.

"Okay, how about 'helado'?" Hernandez fairly chirped.

"What does that mean?" Childs was still staring at the woman.

"Mr. Icecream."

"Sorry, I'd rather be Mr. Apple Pie with ice cream on top."

"You're a smartass, Childs. You'd better get that stupid smile off your face."

"But this is fun. If I'm bound to be shot I might as well enjoy my last moments on earth."

Hernandez nodded his head, tailgating a Thunderbird in the fast lane. "Right. Listen, you just hang back and wait for my signals. Chances are you won't even have to show your face. Still, I need you in case of back-up."

Childs blew a kiss at an older woman in a white Mercedes. "You're saying I'm expendable. Thanks a lot. I didn't join the force to eat donuts on company time."

Hernandez coughed with satisfaction, and took the off-ramp at high speed. "Now you're sounding like a rookie. Don't let Dragnet and Adam 12 go to your head."

"Hey, you're not much more than a rookie yourself." Childs preened in the cracked side mirror. He offered a gap-toothed smile, and rubbed the ointment between his fingers. "Besides, you know I prefer apple pie and ice cream to donuts."

"You brought it up, chubby boy, not me. I just sit here and wait for you to be stupid." Hernandez swerved through a corner, almost touching tire to curb.

Childs raised his voice. "Hey, what are you trying to do? Run over dead cats in the gutter?"

"Do you know that you smell like Swiss cheese?"

"Not really. Do I?" Childs started to raise an arm.

"Yeah, roll down your window a bit. I'm starting to get claustrophobic." Hernandez took a deep breath.

"Why? We're in an open desert here. You should get enough air in your fucking lungs as it is."

"Just stare at the palm trees and shut up. All right?" Hernandez executed another raking turn, and mangled a few fallen palm fronds in the process. "You're not dead and rotting yet, even though you have the intestines of an eighty year old."

Childs begged, "Yeah, I'm wise for my age. That's what people have always told me."

Hernandez differed. "Wise ass, sure of that. Listen, tonight I want you to stand behind me without making faces."

"Of course, boss." Childs gave a salute.

"I'm serious now, Childs. You had better just adopt a stony stare."

"A real Dirty Harry, huh? Anyway, why did we get off the freeway? You getting scared of high speeds?"

"Right. Listen, chubby, you know that I like to take long drives. Besides, I can't drive fast enough on the freeway, and I'd rather not put up the flasher for other patrol cars to see." Hernandez admired the Spanish style houses, with their iron-barred windows and soft, pastel exteriors.

"Don't you think someone would be more liable to call the police seeing a mexi wagon driving through well-to-do neighborhoods?"

"Watch your choice of words, fatboy."

Childs smoothed dab over his left-leaning colic. Too sensible to be a cop. He swore silently at his reflection. The greased up fratboy. Hands spastic in his lap. "All right, where's my sports page?"

"Honey, you're not being sensible. That chief of yours is a born manipulator."

O'Dool was gritting his teeth in the phone booth. He rubbed his cheek bristle the wrong way. Pinks Chili dogs in line of sight, just out of reach. Across the street, a dog curled up into a giant bun. He pictured grease juices oozing onto wax paper, as cars scurried past during rush hour.

"Marie, you don't have to lecture me about my job. Following a booze hound to Mexico isn't my idea of an assignment." O'Dool bit his tongue, but did not taste blood.

"You didn't listen to me when I told you to push harder to become chief. Now we're stuck in a sleazy town with a lack of intellectual stimulation."

O'Dool wondered, "Did you practice this trite speech on your flight? Or did you lift part of it from your trusty Ladies' Journal? He said, "You won't be satisfied until you have a Park Avenue suite and a chauffeur, will you?"

"Don't change the subject." Her voice over the phone dabbled in venom.

"What do you mean?"

Her voice slightly quivered, "This is about you, not me. Besides, I would be satisfied with Chicago."

His stomach gurgled. "Right. So you can torture me at the in-laws. And you can quote memorized lines of Shakespeare even though you don't understand them."

"Don't get nasty. I haven't been severe with you, and I don't want to be. But I just can't stress enough that you would be chief by now if you trusted me."

He thought, "Sure. Have someone else sharpen my pencils. Shine my shoes, lackey." Instead, he said, "Have you ever considered that I never wanted to be a chief?" By this time, his free hand was clenched.

She patronized, "You're confused, honey. Sometimes you need to trust in others who are wiser than you."

"Invest in Charlie's chili dogs," he thought. "Like a hot dog?" he asked.

"What?"

O'Dool breathed deeply. "Look. It's too late to get out now. The Feds have received word, and now they won't stop. It's a shut case and I'm hungry." "Bacon cheese dog for me," he thought.

"Don't be curt with me, honey. I had a rough trip. You could at least commiserate with me before you leave."

O'Dool had purposely called from a pay phone instead of enduring her predictable rant in person. Commiserate. That word again. As is he made the initial gaffe. "Okay, I'd like to hear about your lousy trip, but I have to get something in my stomach before I head to the airport. Goodbye."

No response yet. Guilt complex? Wait? No. Why? He hung up and stuffed a mustardy frank wrapped in bacon down his alcohol-laced gullet. "Ignore speeding cars when you cross the street," he thought, shambling across.

In the coastal canyon, Sara applied aromatics to her body, and sprayed her plants. She sealed her toenails with a feathered brush and frowned at her reflected sunglasses. "Mousy," she thought. She removed the chocolates from the cabinet for Maude, who rarely said "hello" before snatching a handful. Sara bought sweets to help make her content. She unwrapped a miniature chocolate mousse filled with raspberry stars.

"Sara, these are pretty good." Even with the current mixed mouthful, Maude reached for a few more, removing chocolate excess with a licked thumb. "Sara, you really are the best. What's new?"

"The kids are acting crazy and I feel crazy and Dan has a crazy boss."

They shared a laugh. "Crazy world, right? Well, I can't disagree with you. Billy still thinks he's Crazy Horse and your boys Custer and, well, you know we agree not to talk about him. Reed won't harm anyone."

"Hope you're right. Nothing we can really do about him anyway, I guess. The kids keep him occupied." She chanced on a chocolate caramel, and passed it on to Maude.

"Billy really connects to him. He says they're like 'forgotten warriors,' I don't know who told him that or where he read it." Maude ran her hand through her tussled, frizzy hair.

"I just worry about the knives they carry around like forks," Sara said.

"Don't."

"What?"

"Don't worry about them. They will all be fine. I think they just get comic books and life a little confused." Maude licked a wrapper clean.

"Well, it must be a confusing time for them, but pretty soon they'll probably start wondering why they don't live in a normal house." Sara chuckled.

"That is scary, Sara. You can't let that happen. What will you do?" She plunged her hand into the chocolate box once more.

"I don't know. Bribe them with more Ringling Brothers circus trips?"

Maude smiled, revealing tobacco stains. "That's an idea. Or how about promising them a lot of comic books?"

"I don't know about that. Should I support a lifetime addiction? Maybe it would be better to steer them towards stocks and bonds at an early age…"

"Quit pulling my leg, Sara because you can't fool them. You can't raise them as bankers or lawyers. They're not suited for that."

Sara's eyes fixed on a large, buzzing horsefly. "We only guide them, I guess. That's different from steering them, you know."

"Don't get philosophical on me, Sara. You white folk have a habit of over explaining."

"'White folk'? And don't get folksy with me, either, Maude. I'm descended from the Black Irish. We have some legends of our own." Sara's tone was playful.

Maude winked and said, "Okay, crazy gypsy woman. I'll leave you alone. I need to eat more chocolates, anyway."

"Suit yourself." Sara settled back, and pondered some poetry lines. *Long live Fighting Irish. Cherish the day Cromwell's soul rested in Parliamentary dust. History suits the fortunate.*

Sara closed the chocolate box.

In a liquor store in Orange County, Elderly Smith ticked off the seconds. Just as he popped his first high blood pressure pill, Harry sauntered in, hiking his pants up with a rolling right-hip-to-left-hip motion. Smith fumbled for the second pill and reached for his glass of water with his free hand as Harry's pants fell back down.

Harry cleared his throat. "Good afternoon. Give me the best bottle of vodka you've got."

"Well, sir, as you can see for yourself, we only have one brand." Smith's voice was factual in tone, not apologetic.

Harry said, "In that case, give me the dustiest fifth you've got."

"Very well. Smirnoff is dirty, but good enough, right?"

"You're the man, Stan. Throw in a pack of Salem's while you're at it."

Smith returned, "I'm a camel man myself. I'd be smoking three packs of Salem's otherwise. A few Camels will tide you over for quite a while. Pack quite a bite, I'd say."

"You don't say? But I reckon I'll still have a pack of steadies in my pocket when I kick the can." Harry winked once, and noticed how the slant of the sun through the begrimed window targeted the bottle.

Smith squinted. "'Steadies'? Haven't heard that one before. I'm a bit old-fashioned, but then, I do know my cigarettes when I see them."

Harry was jocular. "I bet you could pick the best young dishes in your time, too."

"Still can. I don't feel any older, it's just that they don't respond the way they used to." Smith's gaze was doleful.

Harry shrugged. "Right. Sometimes I have the same problem, but we won't get into that. Guess I'm old before my time, or something like that."

Smith leaned on the counter, and craned his head forward. "You know what I think? People in this century don't have any certainty about anything, least of all the future. Lives might be longer, but life is tougher."

"Slow down now. You're talking about moral certainty. I try to leave uncertain things like that alone. Just drink my fill and have a good time. Philosophy has been dead for centuries." Harry nodded his head.

"Well, certainly, young man, philosophy or no philosophy, you owe me exactly nine dollars and twenty-three cents."

Harry threw his head back. "Okay. When is it due? I could pay you back with my earnings from Tijuana."

"You be careful, all right? One year a friend of mine was thrown into the slammer down there, had no connections, and didn't come out for a year."

A glint came to Harry's eye. "That should keep my buddy straight, at least for the weekend, but maybe you should tell him. It might have a stronger effect." Harry thought, "Who is talking here? Me, or another version of him? Have to get out of here." He said, "There. Keep the change, old timer."

"All right, Cody, I'll pass the bottle to you once in a while, because you're driving the rest of the way."

"But…"

"Don't argue with me. Concentrate on the road, not this bottle. And don't stop until San Diego."

The three o'clock sun was savage.

Ed did not feel hot, but sweat kept trickling down his flanks, as he watched the evening breeze sway the branches of the canyon trees. He repeatedly studied his own eyes in the rearview mirror, as if scanning for a crooked post. Only by studying his own face did he notice the beads of sweat on his forehead, accentuating his baldness. His hands gripped the steering wheel, an unnatural driving position for him, which he quickly remedied as soon as he noticed it; when he reached the junction of Laurel Canyon and Sunset Blvd. It struck him that, despite his inability to afford property in the city center, his humble track house in the valley provided him with ample comfort. He could afford to slowly build a pool in the backyard and plant some trees, and his alternative lifestyle could be safely hidden from prying eyes. If pressured, he would usually explain that, as he was a perpetual loner, he lived alone, which was essentially true since he only shared the master bed with Steve on the weekends.

Sunset Blvd., with steep hills running off its side, reminded him a bit of San Francisco. To his mind, it was this part of the metropolis that felt like an actual city, and not just another appendage of indistinct suburbia. It was on one of these sloping streets that he had met Steve, waiting tables at an Italian restaurant. To his thinking, the younger man was wrong yet right, just like the city, which conjured up endless ambivalence in him. Because there were sections of perfect symmetry and beauty, just like the snaking section of Sunset he was driving through, before it straightened out into an unshaded dart aimed at the Hollywood artery. Even Steve had told him that he, Ed, thought in geometric terms while he, Ed, remarked on the strangely stubby yet pert nose of Steve, as he was fed a portion of fried calamari from his fork.

The curves became less pronounced in Beverly Hills, although the traffic worsened. The large grass median strip was busy with joggers, wearing high socks and tight shorts. Ed still admired the young, nubile female, and even felt a touch of warmth in his groin region. He still cherished the scenery, and came to the conclusion that West L.A. was becoming a prohibitive place, because it was difficult to afford an actual house there. He noticed that one of his cheeks looked chafed, even though he had not shaved in the morning, and attributed it to his sedentary sitting position earlier in the day, while watching Dan smoothly control the construction site.

Baggio's was situated just a few addresses below Sunset. Ed was able to parallel park between a silver Bentley and a maroon Porsche. He was halfway to the green restaurant awning when he felt the first surge of panic, wondering if he was presenting himself correctly, in simple jeans and a Hawaiian shirt. There were potted plants underneath the awning, and a huge vase ashtray, indicating designs toward being upper-crust. Ed himself was against flamboyant styling of any kind, and had even recently hired a couple of architects to rework his and Steve's over-indulgent plans.

From the maitre die's desk, he could look to the back of the only aisle in the dark restaurant, which contained no more than twenty tables. He felt a little unsteady, which he knew was the symptom of a panic attack, but walked toward one of the only five occupied tables. Both men turned their heads and stared at him as he advanced, and Ed noticed the maitre die hold back as one of the two held his hand up in a gesture of unconcern. Ed briefly hesitated, then advanced.

CHAPTER 12

O'Dool had waited inside the huge airport hangar for an hour, cursing everything and everyone, but to himself. He had purposely walked with disdainful slowness when the plane dropped to the runway.

"Welcome, Officer O'Dool. I'm Agent Crum. Strap yourself in over there by the extinguisher. But don't be alarmed. Pilot Adams is firing himself up with coffee, and will be here momentarily. I'm certified to pilot small twin engines, but only in case of emergency. You sure you don't need some coffee, also? Okay. You know, the bureau has some obscure mandate about the daily allowance of caffeine? It refers to terms like "hyperkinetic energy" and "impaired judgment." Deplores the potent combination of coffee and doughnuts linked to cases of excessive police force. The bureau has to acquit itself in a more professional manner, don't you think?"

"Definitely."

"I'm glad you agree. No offense to your LAPD, which is among the best, but most police departments across the country don't look at the details enough. And anarchists are always the biggest headache for law enforcement, because they strive for chaos. Just like the drug dealer we're after…"

"Right." O'Dool drawled the word out with a yawn.

Crum was wearing a cream suit and a pair of penny loafers, with the requisite old, darkened pennies in them. "Yeah, there you go. Those buckles are a little long in the tooth, I'd say. This is a fairly old plane, but it's the most dependable for its make. There is nothing better for its size. A bit slow by today's standards, but the most stable in the air. Adams is a real pro, a bona fide ball-buster, but a trusted flyer."

"You don't say?"

"Nope. We're something of a team now, I guess you could say. I navigate, and he flies, even though he could do both."

"Really?" O'Dool was now safely in his seat, taking note of hanging safety harnesses.

Crum had his hand on his hip, like an affected gunslinger leaning on a bar. "Let me let you in on a secret. My job pays me too much. I used to be in narcotics, and came under fire often. Now I actually have to shave before important briefings. I hope we see some action down there, besides the women…"

"Sure." O'Dool coughed, because the engine had started.

"Good man, O'Dool. Have faith in me. I'm good at the game, and I can tell you know what I mean by that. To make a long story short, I've been in all kinds of tight spots over the years, and I've never failed. Some G-men make a show of preparation, but I'm a firm believer in it, take it to heart. Hey, they won't even put cup holders in here so us agents don't splash coffee on our suits. It's what we call a true "dress down." Hah! Of course, Pilot Adams needs both hands free for the controls."

"Well, as a common cop, we take "dress down" in a literal sense, if you know what I mean?"

Crum snickered. "Good one, O'Dool. I can see you mean to be my conversational equal."

"I mean what I say, Crum."

"Uh huh. Right. Anyway, Adams is on his way now, leaning into the wind. The only thing that is missing is his leather bomber jacket."

O'Dool studied auxiliary electronic controls near the ceiling. "I should've brought mine along. Maybe I could've traded flying lessons for one."

Crum plucked his suspenders, having thrown his jacket into a storage bin. "Not a bad idea. By the way, the pilot is a man of few words, and insists on a proper introduction…"

"Introduce me later, Crum. I'm not in the mood, all right?"

"Excuse me?"

"I'm fighting a case of the shits. Okay?"

Chief Bender tapped his wristwatch and stared at the ceiling, breathing heavily. He seemingly ignored the disordered rows of cops sitting in front of him in the musty roll call room. From his perspective, Fitzsimmons thought he was suffering from PTHD (Post Traumatic Hangover Disorder). His dress shirt collar was slightly askew, and his face was pasty, as if in resignation to the fact that he had been yet once more cruelly denied his fix of deep-sea fishing.

"Everyone settle down now. This will be your final briefing before the op. Tonight will only be a last minute check. I don't want any of you ladies complaining of headaches, because, frankly, I'll have to shove an aspirin bottle up your ass. The department is under a lot of pressure, and I don't need any whiners around. Anyone who does not plan to conduct himself in a professional manner should walk out now, and save the rest of us a lot of trouble."

Fitzsimmons twice arched his thick eyebrows at Childs, and Hernandez needled his ribs, but Childs only smiled benevolently, and swallowed another donut hole concealed in the pocket of his windbreaker.

"Let's be cautious tonight. I don't want to have to find a ballistics training replacement in the case of you getting shot. And, speaking of ballistics, I had better not find out that even one solitary man here has not had his piece checked. Remember, safety for self first, safety for douche bag suspect second. For a difficult suspect, a bullet in the backside will do. A motto is a mantra, right? We will be in total control of the situation, or else there will be incident reports forthcoming. This show will be run like the military, not some wild man cowboy posse.

So anyone who is intent on a pistol-whipping had better bow out now. If you want to whip wet backs, go join the Border Patrol…no offense, Hernandez. Now, Smith here will brief you on the details."

Smith was tall, stiff, and bald. "Once we establish our rendezvous at Sears, I want to assign each of you a post. We will form a circular cordon around the park, but at enough of a remove to not alarm the gang members. I should not have to remind you all about the prime importance of timing in this and every operation. It is worth mentioning now, even though I will report it later, that no patrol car will move without my directive. There will be no exceptions, or else you will have to appear before the review board…"

"Yes, Lieutenant, continue." Bender unsuccessfully attempted to remove a scowl from his own florid face, but is metastasized into a crunched grin.

Smith: "Any rabble rousers would be best served to beg off with sick time, because I would prefer to have only the most professional officers on this assignment. So, Fitz, be forewarned."

Fitzsimmons had a maniacal grin on his sunburned face; ample salt was in his thick pepper sideburns. "Hey, I've been sitting here silent…"

"Shut up, Fitz," Bender interjected. "Speak only when you're told to."

Smith: "As I was beginning to say, Fitz, no rabble-rousing out there. It would benefit you to concentrate on preparing yourself for the ballistics exercise this weekend, and not, well…"

Bender completed the theme: "Fitz, I think it would do you good to avoid gambling and whoring, at least for the coming week." There was strangled laughter in the background. "But please continue, Lieutenant Smith."

Smith barely blinked. "Each patrol car will be given an assignment at Sears. We will be parked in back, near the loading docks. I repeat this, because I don't want any misunderstanding. One car out front could blow our cover. Also, each car will arrive spaced apart, at fifteen minute intervals, to decrease the chance of alarm. The first car will arrive at seven, the second at seven-fifteen, and so on. Make sure your car is equipped with a shotgun, in case we have to erect a roadblock. Now, let's not let anyone get ahead of himself. Orders will come directly from the chief, and only through me. From now, you're all on a dinner break. That's all."

Fitz added, "You heard the man. Break time. Who wants to join me for a game of cards at Harry's Lounge?"

In Venice Beach, Dan's eyes slowly adjusted to the dim, purple light. Before he could wade through the hanging white sheets, and negotiate the ganesha (elephant) statues, he had to reconfirm his position, because the outdoor buzzer did not have a name plaque. Merely a single word: *One.* One what? One man that sits alone in a dark space? One man that buzzes a door? *Advertisement: One chance in life to air your grievances with utter impunity?*

He had arrived at Dr. Aziz's, a friendly nemesis of Harry's who was a professor of linguistics, a foil to Harry's stream of alchemy. Dan had recently assumed the role of mediator in their disputes, but had never visited Aziz's colorful lair.

At the end of the entryway was an immaculate sign painted in red: *Beware of Chaucer. Hark: Tale of a grumpy cur? A canine that barks in verse? Or, a vicious feline perhaps? Advertisement: One chance in life to sip tea with a reanimated writer in the guise of dog.* A ganesha trunk glided across his back and he almost brained himself in his haste to escape. *Epitaph: Cleaved by an elephant's tusk, yet triumphant in death.* "Are you home, Dr. Aziz?"

"I am present, Dan."

"Well..." Dan paused, unsure.

"Of course," Aziz called out in his well-modulated, polite tone.

"So?" Dan took one hesitant step forward.

"By all means, do," stated Aziz.

"Okay." Dan thought, "I guess just continue to proceed with the utmost caution. But what's this lonely cardboard sign in the corner?" *Kindly do not pollute my sanctified halls.*

"Please be careful, dear friend."

"Thank you, Dr. Aziz." An empty bowl peeked from underneath a hanging blanket, depicting a monkey ascending a gold staircase, with a mound of banana peels at the first step. *Advertisement: Eat your daily banana for spiritual steps, but do not neglect your bowl of oatmeal* (he finalized after minute inspection), rubbing his finger along the edge for a decidedly thin, hard crust.

"By all means, Dan, do."

When the hill flattened, the water could be seen (more particularly, the San Diego bay). It was in the shape of a giant teardrop distending from the sprawling ocean between rolling hills. The sunset was deepening the violet sky into purple, but not even one fluttering sail could be seen from the distance.

"We've got to stop," Harry proclaimed.

"You're right. I'm tired of driving." Cody scratched his crotch, and lowered the brittle sun shade, a few pieces falling like dandruff onto his shoulders.

"No. I need to take a piss." Harry was adamant, almost shouting.

Cody grunted. "You're a selfish bastard, barely gave me any of the bottle, and…"

Harry guffawed. "It was quite smooth going down, that's for sure. Thank you."

Cody opted for the first exit, fighting a smile as he vigorously pumped the brakes. The clicking of the empty beer cans behind him became a clamorous din. "Hey, quit fucking around. I know you'd hate to die sober."

Harry was playful. "Yeah, I'll make your ungrateful ass fly through the windshield, then pull the wallet out of your filthy butt."

Cody downshifted. "Alright, alright. Find the first bar, and I'll get you happily soused. See, I can be diplomatic when treated respectfully."

Harry was unmoved. "Right. You're a bastard who only responds to threats. By the way, I want a burrito."

"Okay. There's Alberto's, Roberto's, Adalberto's, Enroberto's, Enrobierto's, Enadalberto's. Take your pick."

"I get the idea, wiseass. Why don't you just direct me to the nearest one? And don't act like such an expert. Stop claiming to know more than you do."

Cody said, "I'm impressed. That is the most complete statement you've made since we left L.A. Maybe I should jot it down on my notepad for posterity."

Harry kept up the pressure. "You do that…hey, take a left at the second light. I've got to piss like a racehorse."

Cody spat, "I figured that out myself. Kind of surprised you didn't piss yourself on the way down."

Harry winked, "No. I have to save it for the ceramic god, and you know what I mean by that."

"All right, that's enough. Just keep it to yourself. All right? You're starting to blabber." Cody controlled his irritation.

"Am I? Well, you know I do like to blabber a bit, especially when under the influence of liquor."

"Yeah, and you fucking drive me crazy when you do it," Cody ventured.

"I'd like you to describe to me how in exact, scientific terms."

"Cut it…"

"You know I could. Hey, there's a Roberto's up at the next corner. Must've been built since I was last here. That off-pink reminds me of Jen girl's bottom," Harry said wistfully.

Cody downshifted. "Your mind's gone. The only pink you saw on her was lipstick."

"Hey, there's a spot! Quick!"

Some twenty miles south, where the arid El Centro region began, a white object slowly detached itself from the heat mirage of a saucer, and finished its descent. When the plane touched down, O'Dool was blissfully asleep, Crum was drumming his own knees, and Adams was pale, exhausted by his prolonging, tightened sphincter muscle (almost inadvertently released by the bouncing wheels). "Jesus Christ, I made it," he exhaled to himself.

Crum daubed at his moist forehead with a kerchief, and spoke into the radio: "That's a copy. Rendezvous at A terminal at trans hub. Copter to apprise us of suspect's movements. We're on our own after we hit the border. Out."

The three men studied each other, Ed slightly shifting on his feet, because a seat had not been offered to him yet; and he had not enjoyed a full night's sleep for quite some time, planning for hypothetical projects on his days off, such as the backyard lap pool he and Steve had discussed over pasta primavera the previous night. The man on the left, in a more staid, beige plaid suit, was in his mid-fifties to early sixties, with a perfect mop of silver hair and a narrow face jutting out to a pointed chin. The one on the right was about a decade younger, with a sunburned, receding hairline, and a yellow suit. His cheeks had deep-embedded acne.

Ed spoke first. "Gentlemen, may I take a seat?"

Gary, the silver-haired one, simply snapped his fingers, and a busboy came scurrying over to place a chair at the head of the table. Ed had barely seated himself when the senior man, Gary, addressed him without losing concentration on his plate of shrimp hor d'oevres . "First, do not be alarmed. I appreciate the job you have been doing. Hey, we've been working together now for about three years. The way things are going, it can't be all bad." He glared at his partner, who was looking on quizzically. "We just need to take our collaboration to the next level, and that's what Molinari is here to discuss with us. I've broached it to you in the past, but now I thought it high time we brought it out into the open."

Molinari broke in, "Gary here is good at speaking, Ed. That's obvious. Oh, and take some of the bread here. Make sure you dip into that oil and thyme. Yeah, like this. Hey, don't be shy, it's not blood."

Gary sat more erect, and a scowl appeared on his florid face. "All right, I think he's got a handle on it. Let's get back to business. I owe a favor here to Molinari, and as a gesture of goodwill I'm including him in my operation. I've got a list of contracts but, through suasion, he can provide me with more." He took a sip of wine and continued, "Of course, the business collective means that contracts should start pouring in. I can't lie to you, Ed. All of us will be working overtime to make the transaction work. Ed, I've expected a lot from you, but now I'm expecting more. And, if you meet and exceed my expectations, we'll make this a triumvirate."

Molinari burped, and covered his mouth with a napkin. "Don't worry, Ed. No one wants you to get hurt. Look at it as an opportunity to swing a bat alongside the big guys. Gary here told me about your work ethic and loyalty. In my business, you'd be surprised how many wise guys turn into rats. Hey, no one is going to hurt, especially you, Ed. We might need to use a little coercion, but no one will be permanently hurt."

Gary broke in, "We're dealing with corrupt unions, Ed. They have their own scare tactics. Molinari here has adapted, I repeat that, adapted strong tactics to the corruption of the locals here. But we need your help. You're a good man, Ed. We have to look ultra-professional, or rumors will start to float. I can't have union stewards over my back all the time. We will simply take our fair share of the pie, no more, no less. And Molinari will not allow any wise guys to interrupt your work schedule."

Molinari continued, "No, I'm out here for money and broads. That's it. Back east it's getting too hot. I'm one of many making a migration west. I joke with my buddies how it compares to the cowboys and Indians time. We've even got the police chief on board. Guy's name is Bender. We fished together years ago. You see, this town is great, because everyone loves the Hollywood scandal, you know, Sinatra and the mob, Marilyn and JFK. Meanwhile, guys like Gary and me can shoot the moon."

Ed remained silent, and made a furtive glance at the red-and-gold menu, even tugging at the tussles along the spine. He patted his legs in an attempt to dry his clammy hands.

Gary resumed, "Ed, I promise you that you can voluntarily leave the group in one year. I just can't let you go yet, and neither can Molinari. If you don't want to be involved long-term, that's fine. But you will make more money in the next year than you ever have. I will personally throw in 100 Gs at the end of the first year cycle. But I'll throw down a couple at the end of the dinner just for starters."

Molinari reached over and patted his shoulder. "It's not what you're thinking. We're the ones that will put our necks on the line. Our accountants will ensure that the paper trail is clean. Hey, Chief Bender of the LAPD will even make sure our path is smooth. All we're doing is picking off some contracts from corrupt unions."

Ed finally spoke, even though he felt it unnecessary. "As long as it's not long-term as you say, Gary. You have helped me in the past, getting my first contractor's license. And, as you know, I will need extra cash to put in my pool." Handshakes were then exchanged, and when Ed exited with a wallet full of cash, he no longer felt nervous, although his legs were still shaking slightly.

Molinari was still focusing on the Italian bread when Gary said, "That Bender guy is something. Some even think he had that rookie cop killed."

"You mean Billy Thompson? I remember him. Fucking walking hard-on, what I heard. Trying to bed all the ladies. But no one knows. Any number of people could have clipped him. We'll probably never know."

CHAPTER 13

The lemon wedge cart wheeled through the dust, veering toward a pair of snakeskin cowboy boots. Cody turned to gesture at Harry, who was standing pissing onto the two lane highway. A sudden gust of wind blew over Harry's empty Tecate beer can, which floated back toward the taco shack. The matron gestured and cackled at the sight of Harry lunging to evade an empty bottle thrown from a construction worker-laden jalopy truck. "Hey, they shoot people like you assholes in Texas!" Harry zipped up readily, refusing to, as yet, turn toward the malicious laughter. "El gringo es un poco loco en la cabeza. Seguro." (The gringo is a little crazy in the head) someone said back in the shadows.

A flurry of feet tapped behind the shack counter. "Me llamo Boca Chica. I talk to all the chicks, ese." A young, wizened face accustomed to cuddling females. The smoothest skin around town. "Hey, ven aqui, chicas. My mother hasn't given me away yet." He flaunted his sparkling teeth and the pristine mechanic's shirt. "Ayudeme, Dios. Mucha chicas, y no hay bastante tiempo," (Help me God. Many girls, and not enough time), he said, flipping some grilled chicken.

"Harry, get back here and finish your fucking taco. We've got to get ready to meet Joaquin." Cody tweaked his margarita straw and threw the remaining frijoles toward a group of mangy dogs.

"All right. All right. I can't argue with you when it comes to speed. You refuse the merits of china white, and, well, it hasn't…just fuck it." Harry spat out the remaining words with apparent disgust.

Cody motioned to the dining bench, its red paint peeling off and attaching to the bottom of their greasy plates. "Sit down. Remember, Joaquin is meeting us here. He's already five minutes late. That's not like him, so it should just be a few more minutes."

Harry dropped onto the bench, not noticing the blob of dried frijoles. "All right. But I'm fucking tired, Cody. I hate all this spastic action. It makes me nervous."

Cody tried to pick a tortilla chip from his teeth. "Okay. Just chill, Harry. Have a beer and relax."

"How? You want to make a scene in the goddamn open of Federalista-land Mexico. I hear they scrape prisoners out of cells after they're starved to death."

"Nonsense. You've been watching too much t.v." Cody added a spicy dose of superiority to his comment.

"Have I?" (scratching the proverbial chin).

Cody finally extricated the offensive chip from his teeth, and said, "Don't be a smartass, o.k.? I'm a bit nervous myself, you know."

Harry smiled. "You don't say. Your having-it-together act was starting to piss me off. Yeah, go ahead and finish that dog taco, but I'd add a little extra hot sauce to take away the bite, no pun intended."

"Sure, but just sit down."

Harry harrumphed. "All roads lead to El Dorado, right? I'm sick of this shit already. Any wind picks up dust and I'll have to pick dirt from my teeth. Besides that, I haven't had a decent mixed drink yet."

Cody shrugged. "I told you, you can't trust the water down here, so forget the ice. Drink straight, or not at all."

"You're lecturing me now, you bastard." Harry folded his arms across his chest.

Cody was unimpressed. "Maybe mocking you is more like it. Don't be such an old woman. I need you to remain calm."

Harry uncrossed his arms, and leaned forward menacingly. "If I embarrass you, tough shit. Never forget that you're only here because of my jalopy and me."

Cody's head jerked to the right, toward the highway. "Right. But I think that's Joaquin pulling up in that, that…"

"Mechanical contraption? Looks like half-truck, half-car. Shit. It's getting weirder by the minute. Would prefer to mire myself in a mud bath somewhere on the border. I refuse to take a ride in that…"

"Amigo Joaquin! Welcome." Cody jogged toward the truck.

"Really, amigo. Is this not my pais, my land?" Joaquin had a vulpine face with a light goatee.

"Sorry. My fault. You're right. We can only hope for the best, being, you know…" Cody faltered.

"Gringos. But this is your partner, right? El blanco, el hombre que nunca duerme." Joaquin stared insolently toward Harry, who was slowly advancing with a shambling gait.

"Huh?" Cody looked over his shoulder.

"The white one that never sleeps." Joaquin said it with finality, sucking air between his teeth.

"I don't know if I like that. Could you kindly call me the Space Monkey instead?" Harry was a few feet behind Cody.

Joaquin squinted and smiled tightly.

"Forget it, Joaquin, he's just pulling your leg." Cody sneered back at Harry, who was hopping from one foot to the other.

"I hope not. What's that you gringos like to say, something like I'd like to choke his chained monkey?"

"That's approximate." Harry's chest expanded to its great girth.

"Shut up, Harry" Cody pulled Joaquin slightly aside. "Ignore him, amigo. He always acts smart…"

Joaquin spat to the left of Cody, whose muscles twinged. "He has to stop that nonsense. Someone down here will give him huevos rancheros."

"What?" Cody fairly shouted, because a huge gas truck rumbled past.

Joaquin made an effort to control his own impatience. "You know, bloody balls. He'd better watch himself back in Tijuana. They don't like donkey gringos like him."

"Don't worry. I'll straighten him out."

"I hope so. Guerrero has invited us all to his hacienda, and he has no time for burros like your amigo."

"I'll straighten him out."

On the outskirts of Tijuana, at an outdoor café almost empty because of the late afternoon hour, three men sipped beer. Crum lightly patted a muscular shoulder, having to reach up awkwardly. "Officer O'Dool, let me introduce Raul Rodrigo Rincon…(noticed the sudden tenseness in the shoulder) de las Montanas. He is a recent graduate of UCLA Film School, races Formula One race cars on the side, and is a fifth-degree black belt and munitions expert. Oh, well, you tell him."

"When I'm with the ladies I'm just Raul R and R." Raul was over six feet tall and a solid two hundred pounds, with a panther-like ease of movement. He was clean-shaven, except for the long sideburns that almost met below his chin.

Crum beamed. "Right. Rest and Relaxation Raul. I like that. Anyway, he will drive us to the drug honchos, what's his name?"

'Guerrero." O'Dool stated it flatly.

Crum made a smooth transition. "Right. Guerrero. I will talk our way in, but don't look at me like that, O'Dool. We will walk back out. Raul will help us ensure that. Guerrero is much too intelligent to start a blood bath. It's why he's been in business as long as he has."

O'Dool's voice was injected with subtlety. "In other words, there will be people watching us watching them?"

Crum frowned, and deep creases appeared on his sunburned cheeks. "No different than any other operation down here, O'Dool. We need cooperation and certain support, or else we're doomed from the outset. I can't be too forthcoming, but let's just say the FBI is grooming for future informants to finger their rivals. To quote Shakespeare, "It's a nest of vipers," speaking of which, Raul here wants it to be shot like a Shakespearean drama."

O'Dool thought, "Huh?" But he asked, "So where do I fit in?"

Raul leaned in. "Think of it this way, O'Dool. Go with the flow. Open your doors of perception."

"Hey, I'm a cop, so dispense with the Jim Morrison crap, okay, or Aldous Huxley, one or both."

Crum broke in. "Cool it. Both of you. Don't light my fire, Hah! Drink your chilled beers and listen. We have to be as professional as possible. We might not like certain aspects of what we have to do, but we cannot become paralyzed by it. I know we are operating on short notice, but it cannot be helped. So, Raul, start revving up the camera engine, and, O'Dool, well, here, have one on me, but just one. Stay sharp."

Fitzsimmons recollected himself, throwing the miniature cocktail umbrella onto the trash heap beside the Sears building loading dock. He shook his head and ran his hand along an arm seam, admiring the crisp smoothness, his jaw smoothing out a mound of Chicklets chewing gum. Where he stood, the corner of the building beside his outside shoulder narrowly contained the marauding headlights of patrol cars. Once the brittle sugar had been chewed into a more agreeable paste, he removed the wad and threw it onto the trash heap. He already had a package of cigarettes out of his inside jacket pocket when he advanced to meet the lights.

Smith disengaged himself from his group and halved the distance. "Sober up, Fitz."

Fitzsimmons thought it an opportune time to fire his cigarette, and expend a couple of pleasurable puffs. "Hi, Lieutenant."

"Don't mess with authority tonight, Fitz. You don't..."

Fitzsimmons seemed to enjoy standing in the floodlights, as if his stage had finally been perfected. "Haven't the vaguest idea what you're talking about."

"Don't interrupt me. It seems that there is nothing in your mind which is not a joke. It disgusts me." Fitzsimmons waved toward the cars to disperse the annoying lights, but there was no movement.

Fitzsimmons appreciated the continuing light show, watching the cars parade in and out of formations. "It disgusts you? Whatever possessed you?"

"Stop the palaver. You can swallow your own balls, for all I care, but get this. Hernandez and Childs are trying to act like the fucking cowboy that you think you are, and, if they keep it up, they'll get their asses shot off."

Fitzsimmons was only warming up, feeling the surge of adrenaline that he felt when he fired his gun. "Now you pause for an answer. Hell, Lieutenant, I lead my life, some follow, and others don't. It truly is as simple as that."

Smith noticed the cellophane inching out of Fitz's pocket front shirt pocket, and demanded, "Give me a smoke. There. No. I've got my own light. You see, that's why you piss me off. No leadership. And copping a bad attitude when you know you're wrong."

Fitzsimmons recalled the first perpetrator he had shot, because the parking lot was similar to the one they currently occupied. He had found it pleasurable in a mystifying way. "Who doesn't? But you're missing the point. I've been preparing myself to retire. Seen too many get brainwashed by the force. Go back into real life like retards. They'd do better to arm spider monkeys with pistols."

Smith was clearly insulted. "Spider monkeys? Get your head out of the clouds and concentrate. All right? You're going to be with me in the lead car. If Hernandez gives the green signal, we're moving fast..."

"Speaking of acting like a cowboy..." Fitzsimmons kicked a bottle cap, which skidded toward the largest concentration of lights.

"Just bear with me. If it turns into a schoolboy assignment, don't dwell on it, all right? I've got enough to deal with as it is. Huh? No. Stub that out and let's go."

From his perch atop the hill, Hernandez could see the Lobos, hands near gun-wrapped waists, motioning for the Locos vehicles to park in their ostentatiously haphazard fashion, some pointing in at a forty-five degree position, some out. Hernandez thought it a sure sign that they were either allowing themselves immediate flexibility to flee, or, rather, simply stubbornly nosing into the curb like semi-permanent tanks. Hernandez turned to regard Childs, who still had his second burger on the hood of the patrol car, the grease splattering on the yellow wrapping, meanwhile bending down to do some last minute work on his bandanna. Hernandez surprised himself by simply shrugging, instead of berating Childs. "Bandanna in one hand, burrito in the other," he thought.

Even the Loco strut was exaggerated, as if intent on appearing intrepid in enemy climes. Hernandez found himself imitating the stiff and yet casual jaunt, chins jutted forward and asses slung low, as if supported by wheeled lounge chairs. In response, the Lobos adopted more casual stances, leaning against their freshly waxed low riders, while their hands crept closer to their pistols. Hernandez looked back to see Childs crushing the oily yellow paper into an oozing ball. "Get your ass up here, chubby."

Hernandez squared his shoulders, and admired the elaborate pin striping of the low riders. "This is going to be your spot. Yeah, where we're standing. From this distance, you blend in with the trash in the gutter."

Childs readjusted his blue bandanna. "Hey, I didn't come here to be insulted and..."

"Just listen. If you hear shots, or only on my signal, move in. Otherwise, just sit on the curb and act like the King of Boyle Heights. And keep the sunglasses on. You won't look so foolish or suspicious."

"At night?"

Hernandez looked around, and found their position still sufficiently guarded. "Yeah, I know. Trust me, it's never too dark for cholos to look cool. Better to be caught dead than with your pants down."

"I think you're nuts to go in there alone," Childs said plainly.

Hernandez pumped his fist near Childs' nose. "That's up to me, not you. I know how these guys think and act. And they're not as rash or foolish as you think."

Childs saw a couple of switchblades being ostentatiously wiggled in the air. "Really? Look at the way they act. O'Dool would beg to differ."

"And you speak for him? Hell, he has his own problems right now. I don't think you should speak for anyone but yourself, chubby boy. This is your training day, not mine."

The three boys squatted shoulder-to-shoulder on the rise above the dirt driveway in the blond canyon, holding sparklers aloft. The tingling of the minute specks touching flesh, and the misting rain, made them hunch forward and pull their hoods over their heads in seeming secrecy. Billy claimed he had found the sparklers in Weirdo's (Reed's) poorly concealed army duffle bag, but his cohorts were unconvinced, feigning to poke him in the eyes, to render him incapable of seeing anything but his Indian ancestors.

Billy threw his long hair over his shoulders. "You guys are idiots. You know why? You never listen, even when it's something important."

Big brother spoke. "Sure, Billy. You can't even fool the little wuss here" (lightly slapping little brother upside the head). "You wouldn't have found them if they were his."

"How's that?" Billy grinned wolfishly.

Big brother said, "He would've been too smart for you two. You never would've found them."

Billy turned toward the rustling in the trees. "Shut up. I think I head something. Almost like a snake, but not quite. Maybe a gopher."

Big brother threw his spent sparkler to the ground, and cackled. "So? You think you can hunt a rodent in the dirt?" He made a quick divot in the ground with his heel.

Billy kicked dirt over his own smoking stick. "I can hurt anything, remember that, Paleface. Because I have the patience to listen."

"Yeah, you listen for farts. That's what you're good at."

"Stop it, guys. No fighting tonight, o.k.?" Little brother furtively stepped between them.

"Yeah, your brother is trying to start one, not me. You want to fight for the last sparkler, Paleface?" Billy was defiant, his eyes like smoldering coals.

Big brother perked up, and his voice played with a higher note. "Let's do an Indian Burn challenge. The winner gets to light the last one."

"That will make you guys want to fight." little brother reminded them.

"Mind your own business, grouse. The Paleface has offered the challenge, and I have accepted. Let's flip a coin to get the starter." He stood up and dug out a quarter. "I flip, and you call."

Yet halfway through the motion he froze, as if he had overlooked something vital. He pointed an outstretched finger at the jacketed figure casually holding a rifle under his right arm, like a bundle of wood, advancing without stealth, directly toward the trailer door.

"What is Weirdo doing?" Big brother asked in as much of a controlled voice as he could muster.

Billy threw the quarter into the dirt, and retrieved it, before responding, "I don't know. He does things I do not understand."

Little brother piped in, "We should intercept him. I don't trust him."

Big brother patted him on the shoulder. "I think he's right, Billy. Let's go."

Billy shrugged, and followed with studied nonchalance. He hardly thought it coincidental that Reed made unannounced visits at suppertime.

CHAPTER 14

G uerrero was captivated by the electronic gadgetry of his hacienda, many nights stirring from his insomnia -cursed bed to emerge in the main security structure wearing a bath robe and bear slippers, toting a gold ice bucket and a bottle of Bailey's Irish Cream. It did not occur to him that his behavior could be viewed as strange, because he had always professed a love for cameras, even where actual filming was not involved. However, he did carry a small automatic in the event that something photogenic crept across a security console screen (then even his beloved Bailey's would be set aside). It especially pleased him to mentally document each guest on party night, guessing the occupants of vehicles as they streamed in through the front gate. He grinned when Raul, who was familiar with the camera positioning, waved.

But who were the ratty looking gringos? "Hector, you believe the gringo trash Raul brings down here? I just hope they're worth my time."

Hector did not respond, because he was not expected to. Any offering would be treated as an unnecessary addition to unquestioned insight. He safely shrugged, because Guerrero's back was turned to him. He was an informant for the Police Chief (his father), but then Guerrero and his father were more allies than adversaries, pitted against the bloodthirsty Federalistas, the military wing of enforcement, who were in the process of trampling the last vestiges of Mexican honor into dust. To Hector, the Federalistas were too young and cocky and trigger-happy to be carrying machine guns. Most dangerous, however, was their notoriously low pay, which created ever deepening animosity toward comparatively rich drug runners. Hector felt like a matador speeding in the cocaine bull so that Guerrero could quickly secure it and maximize profit, then transfer a small brood to his father's palm (he could only hope that his father would not pinch his luxury account while he was still alive).

Guerrero did not speak to the other guards, only making rude facial gestures from time to time, as his mood warranted, to discomfit them.

"Hector, amigo. Do me a favor. Tell my guests I will make my entrance by midnight. I need to draw a long bath."

Hector internally chuckled. Draw a bath? What kind of pinche nonsense was that? If he could just skim enough money off deals in the next few years, he could disappear into the Yucatan peninsula. But Guerrero was becoming more of a constant hawk, even to a degree paranoid; still, Hector had to admit, often correct in his assumptions. In the past Hector would not have hesitated to purchase a trophy car such as a Camaro, but now even the caution of keeping it outside the city limits was not cautious enough. Because Guerrero increasingly employed squads of mercenaries whose only purpose was to prove the ineptitude, profligacy, and disloyalty of his own soldiers. On one occasion, when Hector had discovered one greasy perp watching his garage, Guerrero himself had shot and buried the man just across the fence of his property. "Yeah, draw your bath? You've drawn it already, you pinche psycho," Hector thought, remembering the unpleasant task of hosing the jelling blood off the road.

He ducked under the low-hanging chandeliers on the marble balcony, even though his great height still afforded him a couple of inches of clearance. Instantaneously, a murmur went through the crowd, and one expectant face separated itself from the crowd to emerge with a dramatic palms-up gesture of entreaty.

"A las doce!" Hector thundered.

A qualification was unnecessary. But the host, in the tight cream leather of a matador, squealed, "Escucheme! A las doce!"

Hector allowed the applause to buffet his back as he proceeded back to the sentry booth, past the idolatrous portraits of Guerrero: Guerrero leaning out of the back of a Rolls Royce in a white tuxedo handing change to a legless bum, Guerrero in a surgeon's greens with a Grim Reaper mask performing a heart transplant on a patient with the flag of Mexico tattooed on his forehead, Guerrero immense, emerging from the lid of a volcano with a gigantic tablet of Verdad (truth) in his hands, Guerrero wrestling a bull to the ground with the simple force of his faith.

Guerrero was gesticulating toward the screen when he returned, like a child excited to see his family's genealogical chart. Ice clinked in his glass like a mariachi grind. His slippered feet tapped the ground in a giddy pattern. He was humming the words to "El Baile de Maria."

"I am your trusted servant," Hector said. His arms were disproportionately long, and very loose-limbed, as if they could safely fall to the ground before being recovered. Hector shifted toward the window, targeted by the still oncoming headlights glare.

Harry foresaw events when he bit into the saturated olive of his martini, a fortuitous combination bound to upset delicate mixes. It unsettled him to a certain degree, in fact, that the drink was served from a tray, as if the presentation was suspect in itself. He preferred extremely potent drinks served from bland, tradition-bound bars, where one could see the grit of the past under recent, hasty varnishes, and the irregular gas bubbles floating atop the wood. Here, in fact, there was, as yet, no bar in sight. It was his particular goal to find some solace in the shortest possible time. So he began to elbow Cody in the back to urge him along, thtough the obligatory but necessary Mexican introductions.

"Si, Pedro. Bienvenidos. Guerrero? Oh, si."

"El gran hombre. El que me espera pero me ayuda."

Translation: "Guerrero? The great man who makes one wait but also gives." Cody paused, struggling against Harry's elbow clutch.

"Calm down. Shit. We just got here. Go find a piece of ass or something."

Harry elbowed Cody in the ribs. "Something? You'd better find me something, because I didn't come here to speak another language or hear you drone on about shit I already know. We could be at my studio perfectly content smoking dope." He kept ducking, because arms were constantly raised in the crowd. He felt as if he was evading a giant piñata.

Cody stared at one beautiful mujer(woman) for emphasis. "Lay off. And, you're…"

"Eyeing my martini. And what's wrong with that? Why can't I suspect it of being lighter fluid? My throat's on fire from just smelling it." Harry yelled over the festivities.

Cody relented. "Okay. Just relax. We'll go back to the corner and…"

"There's a bar back there?" Harry was enraptured by the idea. "I can sit somewhere without being bothered?"

"Yeah, but just wait a sec for Joaquin to catch up." Cody looked through the swirling masses.

"Am I being a pest?" Harry sounded repentant.

"You expect me to answer that?" Cody smugly replied.

Harry ducked under a flying elbow. "Yes. Because soon our heads will be caved in, we'll be in a huge cave like blithering idiots, and even my wits won't be able to save me. You want to say 'spare me' but you can't find the right words."

"No. I just know when to keep my mouth shut." Cody turned his back, and watched the endless greetings continue.

Harry replied, "No. Or else you'd never speak. Just give me a drink and I"ll forgive you." He shuddered at the presence of such low-cut dresses and bright lipstick, and gleaned scant interest in arch glances directed toward him. "Still," he thought, "I only have to find one. Merely one lovely maiden for an ardent scholar-suitor like myself. Or suitor-scholar? Ah, fuck it."

Cody urged him with a clap on the shoulder. "This way. But don't complain if the drinks are weak. Joaquin says Guerrero skimps on the booze."

"Then why is my martini on fire?" Harry's voice slightly screeched, because it had gone beyond being hoarse.

"You just have a problem with vodka. That's all. You just need to wake up," Cody muttered, his hand entangled in a low-cut blouse.

"Stop repeating yourself, is all. Do useful things, like leading me to pay dirt."

Their heads turned, because there was a slight commotion near the front door, and a confusing mix of accosting voices: "Hey, amigos, Raul Montanas esta aqui. Here to steal all the women. Si, si, and to drink all the booze. Arriba, arriba, empieza la musica."

Harry thought he was hallucinating, because as soon as Raul snapped his fingers a mariachi band struck up a tune on the balcony, blaring horns shaking chandeliers, prompting lifted skirts. Colored panties were tangy flowers surrounding Raul de las Montanas, the erect phallus, weaving through a windblown female forest.

Appropriately enough, the bar was empty. Even the bartender looked beyond his immediate duties, clapping his soap-scudded hands. Harry blew the airborne scud back at him. "Sorry, senor, but una cerveza, por favor." The barkeep returned a truculent glare. "Claro que si. Momentito." Still, he paused between each step in the beer transaction to update himself on the barely controlled festivities. Raul had a drunk in a head clamp, which seemed to cause the quarry unaccountable and great hilarity, his free hands tapping his knees to the pulsating beat, half-spluttering and half-choking. Raul, as yet, had not attached to any females, but he pointed and winked at a few with a free hand, as if to say, "Wait until I have some, but only some of the animal out of me."

Harry drank half the beer in two gulps. Despite himself, he could not continue to sneer, especially when the last gulp of beer went down smoothly and another bottle appeared atop the bar without a further request.

Cody had been cornered by Joaquin, who was gesticulating wildly toward Harry, and silently mouthing "loco puto" and other choice Mexican obscenities.

"Control him, Cody, or else Guerrero will drink him under the table."

"What?" Cody was befuddled, scratching his chin.

Joaquin raised his voice even further. "Just what I said. He likes to challenge drunk yanquis to drinking contests. It's his, what do you norteamericanos call it, badge of courage?"

"Give me a break, Joaquin." Cody could find nothing better to say.

"Me? What about you?" Joaquin put a finger on Cody's bony chest.

"Huh?" Cody looked toward Harry.

Joaquin struggled for words. "You bring some disaffected boozer, man. Look at him. He's nasty. I don't know how you handle him, but I don't want to know, either. He's too loco in the head."

"Yeah, but he's okay," Cody said piteously.

Joaquin cleared his throat and let his free hand graze some female buttocks. "He's okay? Why don't you explain, amigo, because tonight is business. Okay? I know you and your amigo aren't too interested in that asthma of life."

"You mean aspect?"

Joaquin controlled a curse. "Whatever. There's enough to worry about already without that distract. Okay? Don't bring him back here next time. I'd rather have a Bear..."

"You mean Bruce?" Cody had to correct.

Joaquin flinched. "You know who I'm talking about. I like that guy. He's funny, but also serious. This guy, I don't know what to think. He's sloppy, he's weird, and he acts like he's known me a long time. It molests me." He scratched at his left flank with a turquoise-bejeweled hand. "He reminds me of my lazy uncle Eduardo, who lives on a couch. That's no good. I don't whine like him."

Cody threw his hands up. "Okay. Then let's just worry about business. All right? Because my cash has dried up."

Joaquin did a quick two step to the Texican beat of music. "Hah! It is a tragedy, isn't it, when a man is dry? But you told me that you were bringing me something invaluable. And now this?" gesturing toward the bar in disgust. "That puta."

Cody recovered himself. "He knows a lot of people. If you get me a better cut, he'll move the supply."

Joaquin kept up his negative pressure. "I doubt you, amigo. You need to learn more self-control, because I wonder about a guy who can't even afford his own car. Do you know what I mean?"

Cody protested. "Hey, I just like to spend my money. Isn't that my business? I mean, I like to reward myself after a job well done."

Joaquin started to back away before he finished his remark. "I think you have too big of an opinion of yourself, amigo. You need reality, holmes. Work harder, and you'll get your reward. But go join your puta, so I can think about this in peace."

O'Dool had grave misgivings, but Crum had made him loathe to share, challenging each of his arguments before he could verbalize them. O'Dool thought Crum drove too methodically for a Fed.

"Say no more, O'Dool. I know how things work down here in Mexico. People here slaughter weak dogs, no? So stop worrying. Raul will smooth our way." But O'Dool saw portents in the wildly waving crowds along the main drag of Tijuana en route to the sprawling hilltop hacienda. Some saluted him with the timeless sprouted middle finger while few did not parade a creatively obscene gesture or two. Even emaciated dogs appeared to growl at him with spite and misguided envy.

The sidewalk taco stands, with their rich, greasy aromas, goaded his stomach into deep questioning of the entire operation. Maria's taco sauce-laced lips beckoned from afar, urging him away from his wife Marie's brassy opinions. But then Crum was attempting to blind him:

"O'Dool, have you ever heard that expression 'Being touched by the hand of God?'"

"Yes."

Crum's hands were at a maddeningly perfect placement on the steering wheel. "Well, here we are. Few people, even G men like myself, have the opportunity to view the drug world up close, and it is because we are blessed with opportunity, vision, and insight. All impediments must be immediately available to find the right mix. Raul isn't saying anything now, but he always seems to come up with the right mix himself."

"Really?"

Crum pointed at O'Dool's forehead in the rearview mirror. "Of course. The man knows how to mix everything up to find the appropriate recipe. Slogans can sound hollow, but Raul rounds them out, if you know what I mean?"

To O'Dool's chagrin, Raul was not reluctant to speak. "Si, si, magnifico. I could not have said it better myself. My many travels and experiences have taught me that the only way to view an individual world is through the eyes, the lens, of that world. You understand me. Seguro. You following?"

"Yes." O'Dool's voice was wooden.

"Okay. Muy bien. We are not, and should not be, enemies. I'm an actor, but I don't need a Laertes-"

"Hah! Didn't I tell you this guy is a cut-up?" Crum asked.

"Yes, you did," O'Dool stated flatly.

Raul continued, "As I was saying, when someone works with me, not against me, the honor redounds to him. Hope I'm not being too sophisticated and complicated."

O'Dool stifled a laugh. "No, go ahead, Randy man."

"Huh? Anyway, I have a theory or an equation for everything. I'm not kidding you. Of course, I use the words and even letters as abbreviations, but for women it is very easy, almost too easy. Tell women you love them, whether you do or not, smile and hug. See? Sometimes you can even convince yourself that you do love them. It's really very elementary with the female persuasion."

"Love 'em and leave'em?" O'Dool offered.

Raul corrected him. Exactly, amigo, but you must, I repeat you must leave gently."

"Sure. Ditch them in the middle of the night with a teddy bear and a card and a rose." O'Dool's tone was cruel.

Raul laughed, and the compartment practically shook with the vibrations. "Magnifico, no? Hey, Crum, this guy is finally coming around."

Crum assented, his hands locked in the thin steering wheel. "Well, it's about time. O'Dool acts as if he has nothing else to learn, but there is always something else. Right?"

Crum continued, periodically removing one hand from the wheel to wave cynically at the onlookers. "You know, Raul, the bureau is counting on your live footage to show how drug cartels operate. I think that your work could endure, have a long-term impact on law enforcement. Now that's something, isn't it?"

Raul assented, "Perfecto, Crum. My work will endure because of its artistic, as well as its social impact. The name Las Montanas will be associated with the peak of artistry, alongside Fellini and Ray."

O'Dool resisted clapping his hands, and tried to lock eyes with a scampering Chihuahua upsetting order around some temporary flower stands. He noticed an old woman making the sign of the cross as they turned onto the private road, as Crum meddled with the various settings of his watch, with Raul temporarily silent, as if content in the knowledge that, for the time being, his self-praise could not be surpassed.

Smith drove through Boyle Heights, without a fixed plan. His sole consideration was to keep himself apprised of Hernandez and Childs' activity, but he was reluctant to sit impatiently in a parking lot surrounded by overeager cops like himself. "Commanding officer's prerogative," he thought as he cracked open his window, and scanned the surfaces of streets. Chief Bender had specified that it was "his show," meaning that he would not interfere with the actual operation in the field. He tried to ignore Fitzsimmons' presence next to him by humming himself to distraction.

"Hey, Fitzsimmons, cut it."

"I warned you. You had better let me drive, or else invite me along." Fitz was glaring.

"Don't give me shit with driver's seat crap," Smith played along with the bellicose jocularity.

"There you go again. You know it's customary for the junior officer to drive and..." Fitzsimmons was having trouble controlling himself.

"I don't care what's customary, all right? Just direct me to the nearest coffee shop." Smith was driving almost unconsciously, the trees leaning down along the light-flooded hill streets.

"Right. I'll take donuts myself. I prefer life sweet, not bitter." Fitzsimmons adjusted his seat all the way back.

"Right now it all tastes bitter, right? You think everything is useless, but you're the only clown here." Smith watched a man hold an empty bottle upside down over a rusting shopping cart.

"You mean in the department? What kind of clown? You know, you're just a clown of a different stripe." Fitz was truculent.

Smith slowed, and executed a U-turn, tires crackling over the broken glass. "Okay. We're heading back to the rendezvous. I'm tired of circling like a buzzard."

Fitzsimmons adjusted his seat back to the vertical position. "All right, oldie, but stop at the corner deli first. I need a fix."

Smith was slowing to a stop with the engine off when the radio came to life. "All units, officer going in. I repeat, officer going in." It was Childs' voice up on a nearby hill.

CHAPTER 15

Officer Hernandez had practiced lies in front of mirrors and watched for minute twitches and starts. Full-length mirrors accentuated the casual swayed back look he was at great pains to adopt, since it was in stark contrast to the precise spinal alignment of the LAPD. For weeks, he paraded lies one at a time in front of any available mirror, critiquing himself to the degree of condemning excessive sweat or clammy palms. Shocked glances became the norm around the urinals of restaurant bathrooms as he studied himself in mirrors.

One patron of El Toro's, a probable Loco, had made a fanning motion in his direction with a blue-checked bandanna. Hernandez inwardly cursed at his misfortune, but consoled himself with the thought that the odds of seeing a particular cholo again were negligible.

His mustached face, although handsome, was unremarkable, neither thin nor full, and his height was perfectly average, so it was difficult to attract much notice. His first wife, who divorced him for a traveling band, told him that he was "smooth and plain," like white bread, as is she had absorbed the arguable wisdom of poetic rock lyrics. He was content to conform to the more solid properties of beer, football, and camping, sunning in the Dinky Creek area of his fancied Sierras. His wisdom derived from an acceptance of predisposition, such that could dismiss the frenzied dalliances of a wife who had never discovered her own sensuality.

Hernandez mistrusted people who pried into the recesses of ideas no one could readily understand, or mysterious aspects of life which could only be attributed to a higher power necessarily out of reach of individual minds. So why had she married him? Did she want him to wear disguises? But Hernandez shrugged such things away with a splash of cold water, the trickle tickling between his eyes.

At present, however, a cold Budweiser can had to suffice, applied to his sweaty bandanna. Somehow he had found his way inside the ramshackle house, without being accosted. Perhaps his shielded eyes had provided just enough pressure on the plaid shirts, white ties, corduroy black slippers, and dangling pocket chains, to admit a stranger. Admittedly, he had shaken a few hands and patted a few shoulders, but, as a common cholo, machismo did not allow warm introductions or irrelevant talk or shared beers and joints. He just nestled, back to the wall, watching others follow suit.

El Gato Grande (Big Cat) Roberto Cruz sat in the opposite corner in a deeply cushioned lounge chair, the wind-buffered curtains hiding his shaved head. Next to him were metal tubs filled with ice and beer, which from time to time his hands patted with affection. Eucalyptus leaves blew through the window as well as some dust, swirling to rest. Cruz allowed his nostrils a faint scent of the marijuana warming in his chino's pocket. He stood with some difficulty, because of a chronically sore knee injured in a distant scuffle. He could still recall, in minute detail, the smell of the birds-of-paradise when he was blindsided on the cracked sidewalk, and the sticky stain of enemy blood on his torn shirt. Confrontations were expected, ever since he had been entitled to the title of manos rapidos (fast hands) after defeating a rival on an improvised ring of black playground mats. It was his rare fortune to have survived an early campaign for gang leadership, as friends fell to gunfire, and dangerous women.

"Okay, cholos and cholitos"(suppressed giggles). We're all to make, you know, some sort of truce. So no bullshit in this casa, si? Now that Billy Boy's over, we can work without pigs hassling us. All you eses are bored, no? You want some action, right? So you all have to start listening to me. Or else we'll get more trouble than we can handle. It's up to you guys to see."

Hernandez nodded his head alongside others, wondering about the reference to "Billy Boy," which he surmised was meant to be ultimately unknowable and, thus permanently would be. However, the private aside did not prevent him from depressing the play button of his miniature tape recorder.

Cruz's voice deepened. "Word is that the spooks are starting their own gang down in Watts. Now, just calm down, holmes. The Black Panthers started it all for the brothers. Word is that some of the new members of these Bloods, as they call themselves, are looking to impress, might try some shit up here. So I just want you all to be cautious, because the home front is the key now, right? So stop any spooks around. But no pistolas if you can help it, si? We have to worry about the cops in that case, so we only do it if we have no choice. Hold your horses, holmes. When I'm finished I'll let others speak. I don't want people to think that is the only concern. We still have to move the weed. I won't accept drop-off now, because we can't afford to show any weakness. The spooks have to stay out of our territory. I'm willing to bet my cojones on that. But pachucos here used to lose theirs over smaller bets."

Cruz stood, and started pacing back and forth. "Anyone want to argue? No, holmes? Not you? Hey, everyone is a brother right now. Back out there it is a struggle, no? Someone takes your money, he's the enemy. Someone challenges your block, you have to at least cut him, right? Si, si, sometimes it's that simple, too damn simple, really. Everything is earned, right? Even time in the slammer."

"We don't know about these Bloods, okay? Run by an ex-con doesn't tell us much, right?" (clinking of bottles and cans in a salute). "Hear they don't have anything to do with that Black Panther shit. These guys like to make money and have a good time, like us. That's more threatening though, Holmes. It means these guys are serious. They don't care about politics, couldn't give a damn what some white boys or the Nation of Islam thinks of them. They're above that shit. And so are we, cholos. We honor everyone except the pigs, because they have all the power. I mean, how many cops ever saved our homie's lives? None. That's how many. So if they have a job for us, we'll take it, but it had better be a big payoff. Billy Boy was different. Now we're just talking about our whole business. We have to stay free to do what we have to do. And to get the chicas, we all know that a cholo needs some hard cash. Right? Okay, I've said my peace for the time being. Anyone have something to add or offer?"

There was a slight commotion in the back and hands slapped a back. Hernandez joined in the adulation, and a short and wispily thin amigo struggled to disengage himself, scratching his mustache and squaring his narrow shoulders. "Hey, give way, ese. I've got something to say, all right. You alls a bunch of trouble. Seguro. How do you expect me to speak when you have me hemmed in like this? Don't make me pull the blade, arriba! Can't tell my boys from you rest. No, I can't. And stop treating me like a pup. Yeah, I can bite hard, so watch out."

"So here it goes, Gato Grande. They call me El Grande. I'm sure you've heard of me. Honestly, how can we trust that Bloodies will leave our stuff alone? It won't take them long until they're sniffing our product down at the San Pedro docks. Watching our backyard is no trouble, but the outskirts are what I'm worried about. They're much closer to the point than we are. Maybe we should show them some muscle to make them think twice before invading our turf. Right? They're the invaders, so they have to respect us."

Cruz quickly offered, "I hear you, El Grande. But don't forget that we have a new crew down there."

"Small as they are?" the junior gangster pointed out.

"Please don't interrupt," El Gato said, leaning back against the wall. "They are learning. I go down twice a week to check up on them. They fear disappointing me, which is good. Right, ese?"

"No doubt, holmes. Just don't get too eager." El Gato felt his own pulse quickening.

"What?"

El Gato lowered his voice. "No disrespect, but maybe we need some old hands down there also?"

"Let me think about that." El Gato kicked an empty beer can along the baseboards.

"A combined crew." El Grande raised himself onto his toes for a momentary gain in stature.

El Gato paused for a deep breath. "I said I'd think about that. That's all. I can promise you…"

Hernandez tapped his thigh and kept the smile from forming on his face. When the Bud cans crashed, he kept to himself, but made sure to drink at a more moderate rate, and to constantly acknowledge the nods and handshakes. If someone had chanced to ask, he would have heard that his name was Herm. But it never happened, because the machismo and rivalry kept thoughts from taking verbal form. He finished the beer out on the curb, where other cholos were already gathering.

In the blonde canyon, Billy refused to share the binoculars on the perch of the privy hill, and dismissed the contention that the smell was overpowering. "You guys are sissies. I'm going to tell Psycho when dinner is over." He pushed the competing hands away, and chuckled, "I won't tell you where I found them." Little brother momentarily looked above and beyond the trailer to the road, and thought he saw the rustle of a rattlesnake weaving through the weeds. He reached in frustration, wanting to see the snake at less of a remove, but Billy had already moved away, and started executing spirited turns.

Big brother grimaced. "I bet that the dance is a fake. Doesn't look like the one that Indian group at school did."

Billy sneered. "Whatever. If you guys leave me alone I'll tell you what Psycho is doing."

Big brother snarled, "Our parents, idiot! Those are our parents. You don't care what Psycho does, do you?"

Billy laughed. "Don't worry, Paleface. You saw him place the rifle on the ground before he went in. If he wanted to kill them it would've been done already. But you should both realize that Psycho answers to me!"

Reed furtively reached into his pocket and pulled out a small bottle of parmesan cheese. Out of the corner of his eye he assured himself that the rifle in its sleeve was safely hidden under the trailer. Blushing, he said to Dan, who had already invited him inside, "I hope you don't mind me bringing this. I like to use it with everything I eat."

Dan stepped aside. "Sure. We can all use it."

Reed hesitated briefly. "Uh, yeah, I got you. But you sure it's okay I come up like this? I mean…"

Sara was browning the pork cutlets. "No, it's good you're joining us. We always cook a little extra, especially when the kids stay out a bit. They'll enjoy their share later."

"Those are good kids alright, Sara. Sometimes they make fun of me, but I get used to it." He straddled a chair, and his voice was slightly wooden. "Nice shack here. Easily defensible." Recollecting himself, he shifted his weight a bit, and began again. "I have the shakes under control now. Only gunfire disturbs me. Hey, most of my buddies are back now, so I can rest easier. War's almost over, just hope not too many MIAs and POWs get left to rot." A plate was set in front of him, pork, green beans, and a baked potato but, for the time being, he only sprinkled his cheese and cut open the potato, mesmerized by a private thought. "I talk a lot now, doctor says it's good for my therapy. Sometimes I write down my most extreme thoughts. Doc calls it shitting. Everyone and everything The Shit, good and bad. Take it all in. Brothers call grass The Shit, but also the patrol. A fight with some warning we were okay about, because we had the superior firepower and, well, but you've probably heard enough about us being out in the soggy muck squishing making noise for Charlie, it was all different. Once we had recovered from an ambush, and started firing back, we had lost almost all the good men we would lose. Over in seconds, and we were raking the gooks like no tomorrow, sometimes offing ten at a time, but we could never win. The fucking futility of it, but, hey, that's the wonder of war, right? I mean, how can a war be over when there are still people to kill? But the wonder of this now, that I'm sitting with you guys having a nice meal, makes it better."

"We're glad you're here, Reed." Dan shot a glance at Sara, and continued, "You know I would never come out and ask about the war."

"Yeah, right on. The War. You don't call it the Vietnam War, and I like that. People talk about WWI and II as simply wars, but they try to call Vietnam some sort of foreign conflict. People killing and getting killed as a daily job is what war is, so Vietnam is no different. No bonuses for each kill, just the feeling of saving your own life and your platoon's with each kill. Speaking of which, it's about time I finish off this pork chop." He ate neatly but quickly, with his head lowered, eating each string bean by neatly folding it over in his mouth with the fork.

"We're glad to have you as a guest," Sara said.

"Thanks. You folks are kind, I could tell from a distance. Hope I didn't alarm you guys lurking around, but my Doc says it will take a while before I can sit still. No, it's okay. I appreciate the offer, but, yeah, wine is out, too. I tell him it doesn't hurt as much moving around when your guts are torn out. When on one side you feel like going back to the Shit to save whoever you can, and, on the other hand, you realize it's no use. But those kids, especially Billy, keep my occupied. Sometimes I play along with the crazed warrior thing, but sometimes I'm not too sure."

"You, uh, seem pretty good, Reed," Dan said.

Reed pondered for a moment, chewing slowly. "Not really. It's more like one minute it's okay, the next it's not. You ever feel that? It's kind of like a head blow. Your head aches and you're a little dizzy. It won't go away until you've had a chance to yell. Doc calls it another form of therapy, I just call it raging. Have to say I feel better afterward. Feels sometimes like a needle stuck in different areas of my head. Anyone would rage against that. Still, Doc makes me take meds for it, talks about sliding into episodes and such. Sorry, folks. It's just that people like to forget about stress too much. Maybe I think about them too much, but, God, you guys can cook, best I've ever had. They call us monsters and all, but we lived like hunted animals. Charlie was finely adapted to the jungle, not us. It took time to know I was being watched, like now I feel that the boys are trying to spy on us. Yeah, I'm pretty sure. My antennae are up, so I'd better go chase them, then I'll bring them to the dinner table. Thanks again, folks. And good night." In a matter of seconds, he had stood, and left the trailer.

CHAPTER 16

Guerrero descended at exactly the time earlier decried by the page-"A las doce." Midnight arrived with champagne and hor d'oevres…and cowbells. A few of Guerrero's overzealous lieutenants had secreted them under their sombreros, and the grating noise prompted shoves in their backs from the party-goers. When they were safely expelled, Crum leaned over to O'Dool and related that it was actually a Guerrero-sanctioned event, a sort of tradition that no one, least of all he could sufficiently explain. "They'll be back for the next fiesta," Crum explained.

"Uh huh." O'Dool was busily scanning the crowd, unable to spot Harry, while pulling a champagne glass off the silver tray without releasing his eyes. In the background a sombrero was extricated from the door jamb and thrown outside to the cheers of "Ole!"

Harry had not budged from the bar. With amusement and naked candor, chuckling at the bartender's salute, he kept his alcoholic intake just inside the bounds of control. He started to verbally ramble, and the bright needles of the lights shining off the sombreros pierced his brain. "Hey, amigo, don't you see how fascist dictators reign from the constant flaunting of their fuck faces? Chingaos, no? Isn't that the right word? See your jefe's uniform? Hate to say it, but he looks like a flamer to me. What's with the hand gesture? Makes him look like a puppet. Dictators are usually flamboyant, but not that way, you know, although Hitler did have only one testicle, heh, heh! Fucking diabolical, when all I want if for you to fork over the fucking bottle. Free booze is what I want, not to watch a guy act like a complete fool. The jester was royalty's real entertainment hour. People got tired of executions. No kidding. Had to break up the boring routine of royal decrees, you know, this year the punishment for x being beheading, the next year the punishment for y being a beheading, and so on. The state and person of king or queen lesser divinities. Some people condemn history. To the contrary, one learns about the full spectrum of the human character. Hey, I've picked up a few Spanish phrases here and there. Gives you a dolor in the cabeza just thinking about it, right, amigo? How do people react under extreme pressure? Well, rulers react in several and severe ways, don't they? Go on the attack, to be brief and direct about it. Hey, always preferred English rum to French brandy. I like the fire."

Harry's bar neighbor left his seat and left him to comment, "Yeah, do what you have to do. Don't worry about me. I'm just here to watch the action. But tell my buddy Cody I'm all right. Join me, amigos. All the fun's over here!"

The plea went unanswered. Guerrero was liberally partaking of the champagne and the tall fellow Hector was busy fielding proper introductions.

"Por favor, amigos, one at a time. We have all night. No need to rush like this."

"Me llamo Ernesto. Vivo en Puebla. I have great respect for you, Mr. Guerrero. Because you provide jobs. Some of my friends, they tell me to tell you, you are truly el hombre. They call you jefe and…"

Guerrero smirked, because he had difficulty reclaiming his hand from Ernesto's grip. Hector firmly clamped his hand on the immobile forearm, and finally achieved separation. Guerrero pulled down the shoulders of his matador's coat with a jerk from wrist level, and jerked his head from side to side. "Please, please, hombres, only one at a time. My hand and arm are weary. But, ah, it truly is Raul del las Montanas. Por favor, mujeres, give way for your man. You'll suffocate him in all that flesh!"

Crum followed O'Dool at a slight distance as he made his way over to the bar. O'Dool had already conveniently forgotten his supposed MO. He did not expect anything incriminating to issue from O'Shea's mouth, but neither did he anticipate a lack of all legally suggestive talk. He did, however, marvel at O'Shea's seeming and sudden invisibility. He watched as he flicked beer suds off his hairy lip, Crum meanwhile plastering himself to the turquoise wall between two potted birds of paradise, like an agent out of Get Smart.

Harry motioned to the stool next to him. "Take a seat."

O'Dool sat down heavily. "Don't mind my company."

"Hey, I'm with you, lost my mind a long time ago," Harry replied.

O'Dool watched the women gyrate on the dance floor. "No, what I mean is, I'm not the most upbeat drinking man right now, because…"

Harry nodded. "So you're on the skids, maybe your wife slaps you around a bit. Welcome to the proving ground."

O'Dool smiled. "Uh, yeah, I guess there is some truth to that."

Harry slapped him on the back. "Throw one or two back, you'll feel better. Barkeep, give this man what he wants."

"Double whiskey, neat." O'Dool, surprised by his own lack of hesitation, looked at the picture portraits pasted onto the bar glass.

Harry threw his long hair back and said, "While you're at it, give me one of those on the rocks." He flinched, because the bartender snapped his soggy drying towel off his own hunched back. "I like to keep my noodle wet."

"Huh? What's that?" O'Dool asked, moving his glass back and forth over the slippery bar top.

"Oh, you know, the old clock. Have to keep it well-lubricated, smooth the many moving parts. Left to its own devices, it will rust into inactivity."

"Interesting concept," O'Dool replied.

"No. Proven on the most important platform, my decaying body. But back to your conundrum, which is more interesting." Harry's tone was solicitous.

"Okay. If you insist. The older I get, the more of a servant I feel I become." O'Dool put the glass to his lips, but only had a taste.

Harry replied, "You are right. Do you know why? It is because you are already transitioning into death. But that is also the beauty of it. Sure, smile, it is funny. You see, your body becomes less vital, so you have to concentrate on the seepage of your brain."

"Explain." O'Dool took a real sip this time.

Harry spoke slowly and purposely. "Deterioration stems from the neurological synapses. My theory is that intelligence can be gleaned from this process, if you stop and concentrate. But you have to separate from your ego to do so. Guess I'm blabbing, but I can't help it."

O'Dool drawled, "No. Turkey whiskey makes the tongue roll."

"Hah, hah! Touche! Eat your heart out, Guerrero!" Harry shouted, so that he could actually be heard over the din. The revelers waved him off.

The bartender rolled his eyes in exasperation. "Senor, senor, por favor, please be more, uh-"

Harry guffawed. "Discreet? Of course, of course. Pinche. My fault. Please forgive me. Makes the tongue roll, the groin tingle. Ah, you see where my mind is. Sorry."

O'Dool differed. "No, keep it up. Raunchy talk is always welcome at a bar. If only my wife could appreciate it, as frozen as she is."

Harry raised a finger. "That is unexpected information, Mr...."

"Call me Ernie," O'Dool said without hesitation, a smile appearing at the corner of his mouth.

Harry chimed in, "All right, call me Burt. No, seriously, name's Harry, Ernie. Nice to meet you."

O'Dool shook the stubby hand. "Same here. Damn, it's nice to sit down after a long day choking on dust."

Harry seconded. "Sounds like a version of my day. Put down stakes, pull them up, put down stakes, pull them up." He chased his last sip of whiskey with a gulp of beer.

"I guess it doesn't matter, as long as we can sit here at this bar."

Harry agreed. "Well, surely, my friend. What do you think I do when I'm not making some sculpture? Nothing, that's what. I hate people who assign to creative types other responsibilities which have nothing to do with the craft. Guess I'm cranky before my time, just hitting the midlife crisis stride."

"You don't say?" O'Dool added.

Harry waved toward the crowd. "No. People say get a real job or join the fucking Peace Corps so I can humble myself through wiping my ass with my bare hand. They call that illuminating. I call it humiliating, torturing yourself for the benefit of people who won't understand you anyway. Progress is gradual, you know? Sometimes it's good to accept life on its terms, as harsh as they may be."

"You're talking about direction now, I think. When I can't find a path, the walls tend to close in, all the uncertainty and harshness." O'Dool finished his drink.

"You've got it, Ernie. Got to have Superman X-ray vision. Not to cheapen Nietzsche, but, hah! People say this, people say that, doesn't amount to scat. Think I heard that at a blues club some time ago. No system of life is right for more than one person." Harry was warming himself.

O'Dool looked toward the bartender. "I need another drink to digest that."

"Hah! Now that's a good one. Damn, you're a real wild turkey. Now I can see why you're here." Harry narrowed his eyes a bit. "You're wiser than you act."

"I wouldn't say that."

"I would," Harry insisted.

O'Dool took a deep breath. "You just did. Well, I'm a pretty curious person in a lot of respects. We both know we're indirectly connected to Guerrero, right? I don't think we should have to wonder about each other. It's a dirty business…"

"Life." Harry raised a flame by striking a match atop the bar. "But if you think we're on different sides of the proverbial fence, you're wrong. Which of us knows exactly what he's doing at a particular point in time?"

O'Dool argued, "I do when I'm sitting at a bar bullshitting. It's my favorite activity in the world, after watching Monday Night Football at home with a whiskey in hand and a drizzling rain outside."

"Sounds to me like a good day," Harry mused. "A bad day is when afterwards there is nothing to bring me down."

"Such as?" O'Dool enquired.

"Such as whatever is around. What does it matter? Sometimes a valium will do. My doc has a host of palliatives. I show a symptom, he has a medical plan. Never left without a solution. Old, though. Came up through the ranks in the military. Must have tested LSD on soldiers until they drooled. What do you think he said when honchos asked what Reds were? Imagine some poor motherfucker, drool draining out of his mouth, thinking, pill, no, a commie. Imagine that shit, Bert. A guy hallucinating, just conscious enough to question himself. You know what that's like? Doubt becomes excruciatingly painful, absolutely mystifying. Poor bastard becomes so paranoid he has to be held down when he's given a downer, because he starts to think that the pill itself will turn him into the dreaded commie."

O'Dool felt pressure in his gut. "I happen to know a guy who did some of the video you're describing. Can't say I know him well, and he probably has no idea, but I take pride in doing background checks."

"You work with the guy?" Harry asked.

"Yeah, temporarily. I might introduce you to him later, hey, bartender, una mas whiskey" (the bartender sucked air between his teeth but complied).

"I'd like that. Documentaries are impervious to time. I mean, endless interpretation ruins the best of movies for me. Best case to be made is that documentaries do not require actual actors. Only the camera. Do you think that a cameraman could work well after popping a red? I do. It could give him multiple perspectives."

O'Dool jerked to the side, because Guerrero struck a piñata loaded with poppers, whose harmlessness crackled and sputtered into floating black paper. "That's explosive."

Harry watched the crowd hop and jump. "No, theater is more explosive, my friend. It often falters, but when it is brilliant, it has what? Gusto? What is it that I said? Anyone who refuses theater is not a true actor. They are merely imitators. Imitation might be the best form of flattery, but then imitation is not acting. Because acting has to tap the unconscious. Like the queer military film we were talking about. What was it called?"

"I don't recall."

Harry was more animated. "How about 'Pop goes the Red Weasel'? Hah! How's that for a stinging rebuke? You know, there's the rub. People always like labels, so there you have it. Come to think of it, I always liked the ribbon of Pabst, wrapped around the white can. Like a silky red slip wrapped around a broad."

O'Dool leaned forward. "Hey, why don't I introduce you to the filmmaker?"

Harry assented. "That's an idea. Why don't you just rustle him up and chain him to the bar? We need more people here to be civilized."

Guerrero's face appeared before Harry could properly study it, the visage of the dark, creamy variety that sent shudders through females and caused scowls to indent the faces of male rivals. The shave line of his beard was a perfect parabola. Guerrero simply nodded at him and O'Dool and the bartender, signaling the usual, while two lieutenants studied the scene with casual malice. Harry was framing an introduction when Guerrero took his drink and made an abrupt gesture with it in the air, like a mark of his superiority. "Ah, salud, hombres," he sputtered, then, recollecting himself, strode away purposely. Meanwhile, Crum's limbs were still awkwardly clinging to the wall between the birds of paradise, while O'Dool followed at a distance to retrieve Raul.

Joaquin had Raul's arm in a grip. He cursed at the round, rotund face, which still evinced some lipstick smears, the proud scars of amorous battles. "Look at that puta over there, that greasy gringo. Doesn't he realize that he's a goddamn fool?" Raul chuckled, and smeared some of the pink substance on his fingers, to whiff at his own leisure. "This is business, not a poor excuse for a drunk," Joaquin asserted.

"Hey, what do you care? Your amigo seems to be negotiating fine," Raul replied.

"Ah, si, si." Joaquin saw O'Dool nod in acknowledgment at O'Shea, then retreat. "Let him have his fun. I just don't understand these casual yanquis. Everything a game, an endless game. Directo is the only way to be. The yanquis confuse you until you don't know one side from the other."

Raul seconded, "Yeah, gringos are jackasses. The worst of braying donkeys. But what can one do?" He shrugged. "Say what you will, they do pay."

Joaquin continued bitterly, "Sure, twist their arms enough they do. I don't like having to twist to have something give."

"Take it easy, amigo. There is more than enough to go around." Raul motioned toward the mob scene.

Joaquin wanted a further explanation. "What do you mean?"

Raul complied, "Everything. Drugs, money, women. You just have to be open to pick one of them."

"I pick on gringos, I guess," Joaquin admitted.

"Get your mind off that. You can't beat them, and neither can I. We'll never get California back, you know? Or are you that deluded?" Raul pressured.

"Yeah, que lastima! What a great pity. No more Pancho Villas around. Gets to your mind if you let it." Joaquin pulled a bottled beer out of his back pocket. "I have to drink a Dos Equis once in a while."

"Why this talk? The Indians never had a chance, Americans learned from the British, those fucking polite imperialists." Raul felt trapped.

"Tell me no more. I'm getting too angry, like a hungry wolf. We still get the scraps." Joaquin motioned toward the gringos in the corner.

Raul shook his head. "I'm telling you to leave it alone for the last time. Consider yourself a man first, hombre, but not of any group. It's what I had to do to get over my anger, so I get could out of the puta ghetto and get my life together."

"Yeah, let's leave it alone and get drunk. I don't have time for anything else, I guess. The women wait." Joaquin's cowboy booted feet obeyed with a rollicking two step.

Tables materialized behind Harry before he could comment on the insult to his posterior. Napkins in the shape of jackals were dropped onto the polished, faux marble tops. The mariachi contingent struck up when the ornate, gold leaf chairs were arranged in tight circles. Harry did not flinch, because he could selectively watch the action in the bar mirror, only the bartender's scowl marring the reflection. He caught a diptych of faces in between the bottles: bartender's softening face above hastily straightened bow tie; Guerrero wolfishly admonishing his onlookers directly toward Harry's vulnerable posterior. "Christ, what is this?"

In a patch of lawn lights outside the picture window a statue was being erected. Harry blinked, but the constructors did not fade from view. Fear distorted their movements and faces as they connected pieces of an unwieldy contraption, a bird statue with a rectangular head. Then the lawn lights faded.

Harry thought, "Big Bird?" and repositioned his posterior and smirked as the bartender scurried for champagne bottles and glasses. "Always behind time, huh, lackey?" He chuckled as the furtively pudgy ass became resolutely fat in the bar glass.

Guerrero stared at the back of Harry's head, while a coterie of chicas tittered in the background, hands over mouths. "Look at that puta. He thinks he owns my bar."

"Si, si, jefe. The norteamericano is clearly malo. Bad to the kneebone, I think they call it."

Guerrero replied, "Yes, Eduardo. But let's sit down. That chingao probably thinks we're worried about him."

Crum grimaced in the background, because, from long immobility, his espalda (back) felt fused together. He had a strange compulsion to console himself by rubbing against a bird of paradise plant in a pot beside him.

Meanwhile, O'Dool had retrieved Raul, and led him past Guerrero, which instantly became the triptych in the bar glass of Harry's eye.

The artificial bird out on the lawn grass twitched, then was still. And, just as O'Dool was preparing an introduction, he was interrupted.

"Senores, excuse my manners, but Senor Guerrero proposes a wager."

Harry's visage was glum. He kept glancing at the mechanical bird contraption on the lawn, as if to soothe his conscience that, afterall, something more odd was in the offing. He marveled at the sheen of sweat neatly covering the lackey's face, and the obtuse manner of Guerrero in the background, staring at different areas on the star-spangled turquoise ceiling. It was difficult to fathom, being challenged to a drinking contest, fraternity-oriented or otherwise. He surmised that his crafty challenger, as diminutive as he was, had already taken pains to prepare himself with some sort of antidote, nutritional or otherwise. But his overall mood was, for the time being, passive, since he did not feel sufficiently threatened. Even the potential winnings could not budge him from his apparent confidence. Still, he blurted, "Tell him that I only respond to insults."

The lackey grimaced, and shook his head. "But, senor, you know who you're dealing with? If you were to insult el gran…"

"No. You do not understand," Harry insisted. "The arrangement is that only he will insult me."

"No comprendo, senor. Please explain more in-the-depths." The lackey was dumbfounded.

Harry impatiently offered, "I am not interested at present, okay? Tell your jefe that he has to come up with an insult to motivate me."

The lackey bent over and whispered harshly, "But, senor, that seems loco. Are you sure that you want me to tell him? Because, frankly, I do not know how he will react."

Harry was unrelenting. "I'm not concerned about that. I sense that he is desperate."

"You realize that he is a dangerous man when angered? Do you understand the word 'peligroso'?" The lackey lingered on the last word for emphasis.

"Should I just yawn for effect?" Harry badgered.

"What is that?" the lackey asked, nervously pulling at his own sleeve.

Harry replied, "Never mind. Just tell him to take his time, because I'm not in a hurry."

"Take time? No. My boss is not a patient."

Harry spoke brusquely, "Clearly not. Just explain it to him. I'm tired of explaining myself, and no one else can do it for me, either."

Guerrero sat grinning widely at Harry's reflection in the mirror, arranging the pieces of paper passed to him after being torn from a spiral notebook. It was already clear to Harry that he would have to guess whether they were organized for a single insult, or several assaults. He swirled ice cubes in his glass but did not slow his rate of consumption, since any other course would signal a lapse in confidence. He was mumbling to himself a verbal puzzle in his quest to maintain decorum. "A Jew is a German, all elderly men look German, a German takes a Jew for a wife…"

Guerrero's lackey's tittered from time to time and their jefe (boss) dramatically paused and lifted his arms like a bird's, his beak jutting toward Harry's posterior. Finally, the lackey disengaged himself and sauntered over.

"Senor, el gran Guerrero insists you read these sheets at your leisure. Take your time."

"All right. All right. Set them here, no, this spot is dry." He caught Guerrero's glare in the glass before he read the impeccable handwriting. Meanwhile, the giant bird outside made loud clicking noises, and he knew he was being filmed.

You donkey-sucking, castrated son-of-a-bitch, you suck cow's tits.
You greasy monkey, your mouth reeks of lizard piss.
You filthy dog, your mother raised you on horseshit.
You donkey-sucking, castrated son-of-a-bitch, you suck cow's tits.

"You bastard, huh, huh, huh!" Harry caught himself before he could fall out of the chair, the heaving laughter making his vision blurry from the tears trickling out of the corners of his eyes, his equilibrium completely undone. "Oh, you capital asshole, heh, heh, heh! I'll drink to that."

CHAPTER 17

A week later, in a sweltering and musty projection room at the back of the tenth floor police headquarters building, Chief Bender rolled the film taken from Raul's camera, camouflaged like a giant turkey, outside the main bay window of Guerrero's hacienda, and slumped down in the uncushioned seat next to Agent Crum, who was resisting an urge to snicker, and leave the projection room in shame.

Bender was wearing a fisherman's vest, the pockets containing assorted notepads, highlighters, pens, and a pack of unfiltered Marlboros, which he was at great pains to ignore. Bender attached significance to the fact that Crum, as avid a note taker as he normally was, did not deign to write. Instead, he simply nodded his head, and periodically removed a pen to test its spring mechanism. The clicking grated on Bender, who repeatedly cleared his throat; alas, to no avail.

Crum was determined to distance himself emotionally with the utmost alacrity.

Bender winced at the imposition of the film documentary: flailing arms, bared breasts, and the whirling dervish of Harry O'Shea, thumbing his nose directly at Guerrero and, of course, indirectly at him. He reflexively groaned, and hummed with bemusement, hoping it would unsettle Crum. It appalled him that the agent was not dressed in a suit, as would be more fitting for his professional position. Their awkward scene made him think of seedy old men frequenting smut movie theaters.

Crum repeatedly looked at his watch, his face swimming in the screen colors, which further annoyed Bender. To his thinking, there was no available reason to chart the comic misery actuated by viewing a complete operational disaster. Bender took note of Crum's wrist piece, a supposed authentic Navy Seals chronograph, and wondered if it had been part of a blackmail/heist FBI ransom case. "This clown isn't worth much," thought Bender. "Wouldn't be able to pull or hold rank in my department." He did, however, tacitly acknowledge the high quality of Raul's film, not seeing any devious splicing, and was bewildered by the stunt of shielding the camera with giant bird wings.

"How many times do you have to watch it?" Crum patted him on the arm. "I love it myself. How more authentic can it get, right?"

Bender paused long enough to see Raul's credits spill across the screen in bright magenta, running down the screen like blood. "Why don't you just tell me where things stand. Huh? You act as it's closed one minute, and the next you're insistent about it continuing."

Crum winced when the flapping of the final shot sputtered and made an abrupt move to stand, but Bender had already done so. "It just seems that this O'Shea character draws people like flies. Somewhere along the line we might find someone worth catching," Crum said. "Guerrero is someone we can take down at any time, and, despite the hacienda, he is small fry."

Bender reversed the film. "I think your agency has too much time and money on its hands. I'd love to harass the hippy a bit, but he's basically harmless. A few years ago he was friendly with Pina, but now it has grown a bit cold, I have to admit."

Crum realized that his adversary was wilier than he had anticipated. "Your department will be free to determine its own fate in the matter, make no mistake about it. As a federal agent, I'm trained to see the whole picture. Believe me, I didn't come out here to watch home movies. Right now, I'm taking inventory of every law enforcement org in Southern Cal. I might check in with the Sheriff's Dept. later this month, by the way. I hear their ballistics department is the best."

"No better than ours," Bender retorted. "But I see where this is headed. You will say the complete opposite of what I say, as a matter of principle. I should have been more guarded, but then I am simply unable to act like..."

"I suppose you're referring to the men up on that screen?" Crum pointed for emphasis as the fiasco played once more.

"Whichever way you want to see it, Crum. I have no doubt you'll see it in the way that is most convenient and pleasing to you."

Crum protested, "Hey, we are just the overseers."

"Sure, you dissect our work, looking for the weaknesses so you can prod them." Bender was growing belligerent.

Crum patiently parried, "Why don't you just replay the film? I think I might have missed something."

"What's the point?" Bender stood abruptly and tried to smooth a burr in the orange carpet with his polished loafer, his extended right foot within reach of the flapping film. "Why don't we just relegate it to the Raul filmmaking school?"

"Funny, but I like that, Bender. I was just beginning to think you didn't have a sense of humor." Crum sniggered.

"Sometimes it's occasional, I guess."

Bender started to move, but was detained by the hand of Crum. "Don't get cute now. Just play the film again, but only this time let's fast forward to the highlights. These guys must have been high on something. I just wish there was a popcorn machine handy."

O'Dool's sense of humor would not allow him to consider a rash decision; therefore, the Mexico fiasco edged him toward early (not sudden) retirement. He allowed himself to meander through the San Diego area on his way home, repositioning his dolorous contempt for law enforcement. More bluntly, he saw meaninglessness in every corner, darkness behind every door, even amidst Ocean Beach sirens in flimsy bikinis. To his mind, the proper manner to ratchet back the gloominess was to partake of oysters on the half shell near the cliffs of La Jolla, in an unpretentious seafood house. He refrained from drinking alcohol, because the sweet yet bland flavor of cola made him feel secure. And the thresher shark solidified the oyster base in his stomach, making the rest of his journey more enjoyable. Yet he remained ornery enough to spend the night in the area, instead of returning to L.A. for the morning briefing. He felt unprepared for Fitzsimmons' ribbing, Smith cutting in every convenient direction (meaning all), with the rest of the cops abjectly silent.

Marie had demanded an update, but he refused to humor her biting sarcasm. He threw off his shoes and pants and sat in the bed in boxer shorts, watching the evening news. But soon he felt jumpy, and undressed completely and threw the flower-patterned quilt on the floor and tracked some water across the carpet with a fine slime from the complimentary shampoo bottle that he had spilled in his splashing agitation. He took unfamiliar pleasure in a prolonged shave and a dash of aftershave, and reluctantly retreated to the bed. With slight bemusement he regarded the balled-up comforter concealing the clock within the headboard, and relented enough to collapse on the bed.

His attempt to distract himself with television failed. His personal knowledge of mushrooming crime and exodus to the valley suburbs and canyons precluded it. A thirst tempted him, but he simply filled a plastic cup with tap water, irritated mildly by the latest news of homicides, robberies, and fires splashing across the small screen.

Halfway through the program, he regained his feet and turned the air conditioner on to the lowest setting, catching a glimpse of a tanned female's buttocks straining their Levi shorts beyond the swaying curtains, the artificial breeze now a double benefit. He even caught her honey-spiced suntan lotion scent.

Naturally, his thoughts soon to returned to Marie. She would berate him for an imagined slight, and he would blanch, color, sputter, and be unprepared for a productive defense. Throughout the night he allowed the breeze to sway the faux silk window sashes, yet his anxiety kept rousing him from sleep and prodding him to release his bladder, which only produced pitiful trickles into the brown, mineral-stained toilet bowl. He sensed a certain defiance within himself which he could not identify, an urge to shatter the offensive mirror into numberless fragments, and club the toilet with its own seat.

Morning brought a gradual burning off of the fog, and he was awake, but did not make an effort to rise. Instead, he waited for the dry, hot desert air of afternoon to dry his pores, and the knock of the cleaning woman to frustrate itself into oblivion. He had half-expected an intrusion, since he had draped the Do Not Disturb sign over the knob, which he gathered was only honored when accompanied by low, moaning noises from within. It discomfited him to reflect that, if he had a liquor bottle at his disposal, he would likely not be on his feet for the rest of the day, and that his guilt would force him to make a call to Marie which, even conceptually, he loathed. So, by the time he readied for the road, it was already noon.

"I told you not to eat that orange!" Harry roared from the driver's seat of the VW bus parked off the dusty Mexican road, then leapt to the ground.

Cody turned on his knees to mouth an obscenity, but his stomach had welled up with acid once more, and his outstretched hand hurried back to clasp his wrenched mouth, the cheeks already flapping with nervousness. Beyond him was a shallow arroyo, which looked like a dried gutter of excrement, and a solitary rider creeping away in the distance.

"Come on, puke yourself out. I need to get out of this God-forsaken place, or else…" Harry looked at the mounds of cacti alongside the road, and his skin prickled uncomfortably.

"What" Cody was able to moan.

Harry winced, and cursed under his breath. "What place? Which place exactly should I quit?" It was enough to make him return to the van for the bottle of whiskey on his bowlegged, shaky legs. "This place can really get me down, I tell you that much."

"You hear me, Cody? Don't turn green. You're not going to die yet, unless you want me to crack this bottle over your head? Just let me lean against my jalopy in peace, all right? I don't want you to force your tonsils out."

The horse rider had pivoted into profile. Adorned with a yellow-and-black lightning serape, he cackled like a hyena, and carefully adjusted his sombrero. "Ay, ay! All you puto norteamericanos take el vomito. Viva the curse of Montezuma!" Then the grin turned down his square face. "That's all you ever leave us, right? The regurgitation of what you have stolen?" He pinched his nose and rode off.

"Hey, why don't you just stick your finger down your throat?" Harry suggested.

Cody rested on his haunches, and managed to sprout his middle finger. He picked weed burrs out of his loose, dirty high socks, and summoned a wail: "Oh, ye gods, spare me the curse of Montezuma," which Harry could not hear through the spider-cracked glass, hands scrambling for purchase of the bottle. Cody used his forearms as levers to rise from the befouled ground. "I promise you, you're in for it." With his knees half-bent, he lunged forward, but his balance was inadequate, forcing his weight to overturn him. The force of the impact sent shivers of pain up through his hands to his forearms, and he landed awkwardly on his elbows. "You have caused me too much pain, asshole. I think I should retire you as a friend."

He imagined Harry's lips forming the words "Is that so?" out of a compulsion to have the proverbial final word of remonstration. What he certainly did see was the sudden mouthing of the word "Fuck" after a too lengthy gulp from the bottle, and the hasty rubbing of eye sweat out of their reddened corners.

Cody vaguely recalled a Guerrero sympathizer throwing a large rock at the windshield as they exited the hacienda, and Joaquin, amid the bustle, waving them frantically onward while being choked by a lace brassiere.

Harry yelled, "Come on! Get in, and you'll feel better. I promise you. The ride will rattle the rest out. Yeah, now! When do you think I want to leave, fool?" He kicked some dirt and reclaimed his seat, closing his eyes and leaning back with feigned pleasure. He put the long, knobby gearshift in neutral, and revved the wheezing engine.

Cody finally gained his feet, and stumbled forward. The grapefruit-sized welt he had sustained from being thrown against the bar was throbbing and his eyes blinked in misery from minuscule collections of dust.

"Come on! I won't shed a tear for you!" Harry yelled, gunning the engine.

As a matter of record, Hernandez's recording of the Lobos and Locos parlay was sealed within a manila envelope and deposited in the Hall of Records in downtown on Hope St. It would have gone directly to clerk Dobson's desk, but he was on administrative leave, the victim of the vagaries of governmental budgeting. He had left a terse note unceremoniously affixed with masking tape atop his molding mahogany desk: "I'm out of here, suckers!"

Only Smith took casual umbrage to it, promising to personally demote Dobson to file clerk when he returned in two weeks (Dobson did not mind, since he was essentially a glorified file clerk as it was). In the meantime, Fitzsimmons and Hernandez were too busy preparing for the ballistics training and extravaganza to take notice, opting to deride Smith's lack of sympathy: "What do you mean? At least he isn't calling us Dudley Do Rights and White Peckerwoods and Honky Motherfuckers and I can't remember what else." Fitzsimmons assumed that it was really Dobson's untidy desk that upset Smith, but Hernandez objected, opining that it was because Dobson, a husky black man, was rumored to tomcat with white women, especially young ones when he had the opportunity.

"Don't give me that crap, Handy." Fitz's voice had an extra edge to it. "None other than Smitty himself has been the one spreading that baseless rumor."

"Then why doesn't Dobson make himself clear?"

Fitz chuckled, but there was bile in his voice. "Because, amigo, he likes to see Smitty in a huff. Old Dobsy isn't as dense as a steel beam, you know. The man reads like a maniac, and quotes Shakespeare."

"What?" Hernandez could not contain his shock.

"The man is twice as intelligent as Smitty, okay? But let's leave it at that for now. I've got a hankering for a Wiener Schnitzel dog." Fitz was already loping away.

Hernandez whistled. "You're kidding. You always rib Childs for going there and now you..."

Fitz lobbed the words over his shoulder. "Yeah, yeah. I know. But he eats twice the amount. I think he gets every fifth dog free. Bastard should shill them on t.v. or something."

Fitzsimmons held the elevator door with one hand and jabbed at Hernandez's shoulder with the other. "Keep that arm steady now. No stray bullets out on the range, right? I've heard you've been known to be wild at times, and we don't need any more of those types because we have me. Word is that that FBI idiot Crum is going to grace us with his august presence."

"Are you saying we should put on a show?" Hernandez pressed the Close Door button and looked up at the red indicator lights, resting his back against the tan, ribbed carpeting of the elevator wall.

"I don't care one way or the other, to be honest," Fitz resumed. "He'll probably just show for the marksman competition. Bender says he has a foul mouth, by the way."

"No kidding? Aren't G men supposed to be more careful?" Hernandez whistled once more, which he knew annoyed Fitzsimmons.

"Yes. So he's nuts. What's new about that? He dumps a Mexican headache on us and we're supposed to smile about it? I for one, don't agree."

Hernandez tapped the carpeted wall. "I wouldn't beg for anything. They're nerds with guns, right, Fitz?"

Fitz giggled. "Unfortunately, yes. Every fifth one likes to quote the official handbook when discussing a criminal case. Retards, that's certain."

Hernandez depressed the elevator button once more, which was known to stick. "Sounds lame to me, Fitz."

"Good point, Handy. But you should leave that demon elevator button alone. You know the damn thing is prone to stick."

Hernandez raised a finger. "Just call me the Magic Finger man."

"You're of my stripe, Handy. You like tank top women with big tits. Any flavor is fine with me. Damn, they trying to break our necks with this floor wax? I'd better add some traction to my shoes tomorrow. Remember, we meet at the range tomorrow at nine sharp." He demonstratively ran his loafer across the floor once more before stepping out, nodding regally at the young blonde receptionist.

CHAPTER 18

When Dan left Dr. Aziz's, his stomach was troubled by the lamb curry mixed with spinach, so he stopped at the convenience store on Ocean Ave. to purchase Antacid. It was then that he remembered the unarguably volatile addition of a mango and yogurt shake, not to mention the consternation caused by Aziz's contention that Harry had fondled his (Aziz's) revered ganesha (elephant) statue during his last visit. Dan thought the charge absurd, especially in light of the fact that an identical statue had a strange tendency to fondle him (Dan). But Aziz's opinion was not to be swayed through outside interference, and Dan could not seriously defend himself against an elephant's advances, so he left the matter unresolved, to be taken up later between Aziz and Harry.

Harry and Aziz were often at loggerheads over who possessed more authority over a particular subject. Aziz played the role of imperial empiricist, relying on hard data, while Harry instigated him with esoteric improvisation, tempting Aziz to disprove his various theories. He always kept slightly ahead of Aziz, pestering him with letters filled with arcane and lewd jokes. Aziz's wife, Amina, a linguistics professor at UCLA, called him "that dreadful, horrid man," although she was secretly intrigued by his intelligent charisma. Aziz tried in vain to keep the letters to himself, but he would splutter upon opening the daily mail in the reading room before dinner. "That incorrigible monkey, he thinks he is brilliant. Some day I will expose him as the plagiarizing philanderer that he is."

"Now, now, dear husband," Amina placated. "Do not let your temper get a hold of you, because…"

Aziz's eyes widened. "Yes, I know, the snake does bite! Could you please refrain from your homilies tonight? I am drained."

Amina adjusted her yellow-and-green sari across her shoulders. "Are you? Sorry, retired emeritus professor, but I had to fill in for an ill colleague, pick up the laundry, and a meal on the way home, not to mention enduring the accursed smog of this place."

Aziz reached for his tea cup. "Compare it to Bombay, love, and you won't fret. I must admit that I like this strange place. And the ocean is spectacularly beautiful."

Amina laughed shortly. "You divert yourself, and I toil. But phases come, and they go. Right? Some day I'll have you put to work again." She winked.

"But I'm working on my Magnus opus," Aziz protested.

Amina coyly responded, "Which one? And don't look at me like that. I think that you'll be published soon, and then there will be no hope for you anymore in avoiding the limelight."

"You mean become one of your colleagues at UCLA."

"You're more than that already, you know." Amina said.

Aziz was captivated. "Hah! Very good. Anyway, Dan invited us up to the canyon for the Independence Day event, or Fourth of July? Ah, why fret over details? And don't look at me like that. I can behave alongside Harry when I want to."

Amina dropped a lump of sugar in his tea, and the splash caused a large drop to snuggle in his lap. "That's what I'm afraid of. Perhaps you should practice being more conciliatory toward him?"

Aziz was outraged. "What? That man lords over his Ivy League past, even though it probably can't be verified. Someone has to step forward and teach him some manners. Right?"

Amina used a soothing tone to complement the tea. "Let it be someone else this time. I would like to enjoy the scenery."

Aziz paused briefly. "I see. You call him a horrible man, yet you refuse to side with your husband. I apologize if I'm making a judgment by calling it illogical, but sometimes you sound too…"

"Diplomatic?" Amina spun in her sari and sat down beside him. "Why must you constantly fret? Give me a kiss and you'll feel better."

Aziz grunted. "No, we'll both feel better. Thus, by all means." His favorite expression remained on his breath for some time after their passion cooled.

O'Dool had barely poured a glass of whiskey on his deck when the phone rang. He shrugged, calming himself with the thought that at least his shoes were off; and he only had to reach back to raise the phone to his ear. He kept the television on, but turned the volume down, tapping his knee unconsciously, because he was concerned that Marie could walk in at any moment.

Hernandez's voice was scratchy and a bit dull, as if he had been yelling. "Hey, O'Dool, I think I've got something."

O'Dool was unimpressed. "Not good enough. Do you have something or not? I just got back from a fiasco in Mexico. I feel like I chased a headless chicken through Tijuana, I have no idea why I'm in the force anymore, and you call me to tell me about?"

"Would later be okay?"

O'Dool breathed slowly. "No. Go ahead. My thought is that you weren't shot last night, and neither was Childs, or else someone else would be calling."

Hernandez shrugged. "No, nothing like that. No barrio shootout. The Lobos and Locos are scared of the brothers, you know?"

"Okay, now you're talking. Keep it going." O'Dool's eyes fastened onto the largest of the squirrels tangling in the underbrush below the deck.

Hernandez began, "They want to see what they're up to."

"Okay, so they're putting out feelers. What else?" O'Dool was impatient once more.

"Nothing." Hernandez's voice was hollow.

"What?" O'Dool stood and worked his jaw. "That's why you called? You're trying my patience." The jarring of his body caused his hand to tremble, and some whiskey to overspill onto the brown shag carpeting.

Hernandez patiently continued, "No, that's not the important point. There was something Gato Grande said. I didn't think much of it at the time, but the way he said it seemed weird. I don't know, it's probably just…"

"Go ahead, just think it through." O'Dool rubbed his eyes.

Hernandez said, "He didn't say much, but he mentioned something about 'Billy Boy.'"

"Are you kidding me?" O'Dool sat upright and thought, "Billy has finally returned from the dead, afterall."

"No." Hernandez's voice was flat.

O'Dool's voice became sharp. "That's what the former chief called a young recruit. Yeah, back at that beach party, where everyone was smashed. A kid with a lot of dash. You wouldn't know, because it was before you transferred to Rampart."

"You talking about Billy Thompson?"

"Bingo, Handy. It didn't get out to the public, but it couldn't help but be thrown around to other stations, right?" O'Dool felt nervous excitement surge in him.

Hernandez assented. "No. Word was that he rubbed a higher-up the wrong way, that he had some crude dirt on someone, that he might rat, and that's why he was offed in the desert."

O'Dool refilled his glass, but only stared at it for the time being. "Okay. Good. This could be something, but we've got to assess the risks. And what might we uncover? Corruption? Okay. But murder? Maybe Billy was involved with the Locos and owed them too much. Let's not assume anything in particular. You can't do this without some sort of plan."

Hernandez swallowed hard. "I hear you. If we're quiet about it, we might be able to come up with something. I'm tired of the FBI dictating to us."

O'Dool watched the squirrels run. "Ah. That's music to my ears. Makes me want to finish this bottle. Hernandez, I've got a pulse again. We'll talk tomorrow in person. We can't discuss this over a line after tonight. Can't be too careful with something like this."

Hernandez sounded appeased. "No one wants an early grave, right?"

"Least of all Billy," O'Dool said. "There were too many women to chase. I figured he would eventually be killed by a jealous girlfriend or boyfriend, or at least hospitalized, just like old Robert Johnson."

"Huh?" Hernandez was nonplussed.

"Robert Johnson. Black guy back in the 20s, King of the Delta Blues, one of the best recordings ever. Bluesman. Played guitar and sounded like at least two other people playing alongside him. Had a way with the ladies, too. One young wildcat poisoned him, and that was it. Too much alcohol on my tongue now. I might have to even tell off my wife when she gets back. Yeah, life's a bit of a bitch since we last chatted. Seems like I'm trying to watch other peoples' backs, but no one is watching mine."

"I'll watch yours."

O'Dool watched the squirrels quarrel through loud chatter, competing incessantly for choice nuts. "We'll watch each other's. I'll be, but hey, let's hold it a minute. It always takes me a day to make a decision. This is too rash…"

Hernandez was less hesitant. "Let's go for it. We've got nothing to lose, and we'll be careful enough about it to not raise an alarm."

O'Dool urged, "Like I said, we'll talk tomorrow, after ballistics. But don't even make a hint to Fitzsimmons. He smells plots, that bastard. He has to be at the center of everything, or he goes crazy."

"This is going to be big," Hernandez began.

"Let's keep it small for the time being," O'Dool interrupted. "I need to prepare myself for whatever comes."

"That doesn't sound right to me."

O'Dool laughed. "No, you're right. But I can't help but try to be somewhat cautious." He felt the stirrings of a headache after he replaced the receiver. He thought, "Damn. With the O'Shea business dying, there might actually be room to be productive, and solve a real case."

CHAPTER 19

Fitzsimmons kept the motorcycle boots in a special compartment of his closet. In order to reach them, he had to move aside a small, swinging door that provided a perfect recess in the back of the closet wall. Stooping forward, he temporarily caught his earlobe on a protruding hangar, and almost tore it in his haste to release it. After swabbing it with a moist thumb, he realized that it had not come to apparent harm; so he knelt and picked up the white cotton gloves off the gray carpet.

He had not been on a motorcycle since that distant night ten years before, with Betsy sitting behind him, the nails of her interlocking fingernails scratching his chest as they negotiated Mulholland Drive with the combined fuel of beer and whiskey. Betsy had promised him a night of open fantasy on their previous date to the drive-in.

But an oil slick intervened, fishtailing the bike as they knifed around a turn. He was able to keep his hands locked onto the handle bars, but he felt the nails scratching his chest, and the sudden lessening of weight as they slid toward the sheer drop, because Betsy had slammed into the guardrail.

When he reached her after crawling over, she was laying on her side, staring at him fixedly. He thought she was merely unconscious when he nudged her shoulder. She rolled over to reveal the other side of her skull completely crushed. He was stirred by the sight of her dress above the knee revealing the high boots he had bought for her on their first date. It struck him that he needed something to remember her by, and his bloody, sticky hands reached for the first zipper. He was interrupted removing the second boot by the screeching of tires, the glare of lights and frozen faces. He remembered seeing a young man he would later know as Billy Thompson, tall and lean in denim, striding toward him. Then he temporarily blacked out.

Billy brought a beach towel from his back seat, and together they were able to wrap it around Betsy's head. Billy had wondered aloud about the appropriateness of the action, but Fitzsimmons said, "Fuck it, kid. I'm a cop. I'll tell the paramedics and cops what we did." Billy was muttering "Jesus" under his breath periodically, as the blood kept soaking the towel. Fitzsimmons noticed that Billy was wearing a red-and-white letterman's jacket. Billy himself was thinking to himself that the body was that of a large animal, not a person, in order to keep his composure.

Fitzsimmons held her hand in the back of the ambulance as it became cold, wondering if the paramedics thought she was his daughter, instead of his girlfriend.

He stared and blinked, but the tears stubbornly continued to trickle out of the corners of his eyes. Because he feared soiling the white, pristine gloves, he awkwardly raised his elbows to eye level. It was exactly ten years since the day of Betsy's burial, a scene of ferocious sunlight and arid pleasantries exchanged over the sod, such as "You were lucky, Bob. She could have chosen any man, but she had you." But what? "What?" he said aloud, and laughed off key, the sound coming from the back of his throat, to emerge as a spluttering cackle. "What if I needed her desperately? Afterall, every other guy in the fucking universe did." He slapped his palms together, and turned to admire the shiny boots in the mirror. "I'd like to show you off today, Betsy," he said.

Onlookers had commandeered the road, slowing and waving cars along, although a couple furtively approached the body, until Fitzsimmons vigorously waved them off.

"Come on," he pleaded. "Give us some room. Hey, kid…"

"Yeah?" Billy stood, trying to shield the body as much as possible. "What can I do?"

Fitzsimmons turned his back to admire the shimmering city lights, hearing the first glimmer of sirens. "Nothing will be the same after tonight."

Hernandez motioned for Childs to grab a bottle of green sauce while he carried the tray of tacos and sodas to the only patio table with substantial shade. He transferred the tray to his left palm and flicked some jalapeno seeds off the red plastic seat. Maria had treated him with respect, but had reserved her especially pouting red lips for Childs, who stood in amazement, speechless. Hernandez sipped his soda and momentarily watched the traffic, then shifted his gaze to Childs, who had almost eaten half of the first taco in one bite, the lettuce and grated cheese overflowing onto the margins of the paper plate.

Hernandez was direct. "What do you think happened the other night?" He clamped his jaw shut around the ice from the first gulp of soda.

Childs jerked a little. "What do you mean? You told me what happened inside. I was busy keeping a low profile around the other pachucos…"

Hernandez interrupted, "Right. As long as you kept your mouth shut we were okay. Yeah, keep sweating. I've got more to say. But you've got to answer later, because you've been too quiet."

"Uh-huh." Childs seemed completely unconcerned.

Hernandez pressured, "It's not like you accept official versions, and…"

Childs took umbrage. "What? Are you working in Internal Affairs now? I didn't become a cop to be interrogated."

Hernandez held up his right fist. "Be quiet. I told you that you'll have your time to state your case."

"What case?" Childs returned.

"Enough. Don't interrupt me again, or I'll stuff a jalapeno pepper up your nose. I've never had to sneeze one out, but I don't think you should risk it, either. Might lead to a bloody nose, you know, man?" Hernandez took another gulp of soda and resumed, "You didn't hear anything about what was said inside, except from me?"

"No, should I have?" Childs flashed a fleshy cheek.

"I'm asking the questions here. I want to make sure that there is not any information that you have left out. All right? We're partners, but you seem to want to keep your hands clean. And, listen, I'm all for that in most cases, but I'm also willing to take calculated risks. Are you?"

Childs blinked, and wiped some sweat from his brow. "What is this about? All right, sure I am. Working the beat was boring after a while. That's why I became a detective."

Hernandez relaxed a bit. "Good. Then you would recognize something that doesn't add up. But, other than that, would you come to me with the news?"

"Sure I would. That's why we're partners. Hey, why didn't you conduct this interview before we were assigned to each other? If you're talking about cracking a case, I'm all for it. Is this what it's all about? I mean, what did you see and hear?"

Hernandez's teeth cracked through a taco shell, and he chewed slowly. He smiled, and remarked, "What did I see and hear, Childs? Well, just what my report said. Anyway, hurry up. I've got to get to the exhibition place with Fitzsimmons in a few minutes."

Fitzsimmons did not hesitate to put on the cowboy costume in the police locker room in preparation for the ballistics exhibition, but Hernandez was more reluctant. "I'm no fucking bandit," he muttered to himself, watching Fitzsimmons admire his leggings, chaps, and cream-colored Stetson in the full-length vanity mirror provided by Chief Bender's wife Peggy. "At least the could have provided a Mexican sombrero." He resented the tenor of the competition after the staid professionalism of the ballistics training.

Fitzsimmons was jocular. "Hey, come one, Handy. Loosen up. This is the reward for your hard work." He cocked the hat slightly to the left, and did a little two step. "Don't worry. I'll beat you, but I won't humiliate you."

"Right, Fitz. You just want me to make a fool of myself." Hernandez cursed under his breath.

"Never," Fitz said. "Look, it's just a show for the old-timers and kids."

"Won't happen." Hernandez was a bit surprised by the slightly severe tone of voice he had adopted, insofar as he had always deferred to his superiors to the utmost. And what was that departmental maxim? "Guard your partner's life like it's your own."

"So we're fucking cowboys, Handy. So what? It is for the department's p.r., that's all. And what if we're to be objects of ridicule for the rest of our professional days…"

"Easy for you to say," Hernandez offered. "You're much closer to retirement than I am. Jokes will continue to be made at my expense."

Fitzsimmons punched his shoulder. "You don't say? Hey, regardless of my upcoming retirement, I'll thumb my nose at the cheeky bastards, that's what I'll do. Yeah, I'd like to put a bullet between the eyes of a few. Still, I'll make their wives moist and their kids laugh. What better revenge?"

"You're sicker than I thought, Fitz. How do you keep a straight face?" Hernandez slammed the locker door and applied the padlock.

Fitzsimmons briefly aimed the pistol loaded with blanks at Hernandez's back. "Just as sick as I need to be. Some rules can't be broken, but they can be ridiculed. That's the important distinction. Don't worry so much about being in lock step. All conformity gets is a bunch of boats and houses, but, hey, it's the cowboy way, right?"

Hernandez looked pointedly at their feet. "Okay, but then where are the spurs?"

Fitzsimmons played along. "Nope. Might catch on the saloon steps. They don't want things to get absurd, you know?"

"Of course not." Fitzsimmons strode forward.

"Now you're getting in the mood. It should get ugly." Fitzsimmons added emphasis to the final word, and slapped his haunches. "Let's make them forget the Big Valley." The slanting shadow of the door kept his face obscured for a moment.

Hernandez punched a locker. "Ugly we'll be then. Call me Pancho."

Banners greeted them out on the training ground, a converted high school football field. Close inspection would afford a view of the fading, bulging eye of the Horny Toad Hollywood High mascot stenciled onto midfield. As yet, the peeling paint bleachers were empty, but a voice blared from a hidden speaker nonetheless. "Hey, you folks ready to watch these fellas unload their six guns? Hey, look sharp. This is a rehearsal. You're acting dumb, but I know you all are concerned. This type of event doesn't come around every year, you know. Come on, act like you can walk bowlegged at least. John Wayne was so drunk he fell off his horse but even he could walk bowlegged! No, roll your hips, or else you'll kick up too much dust! I want you guys to be photo worthy afterward. Hey, I know you guys don't want to disappoint the future mayor!"

Fitzsimmons gestured violently, upward toward the sound, and remarked to Hernandez, "Bastard is being facetious. Bender couldn't be mayor, because he might actually have to work. Scary thought, huh? He's trying to scare us into believing this charade is actually important to him. I'm just trying to figure out something to throw him and the rest for a loop."

Hernandez did a circle on his feet. "I don't know, Fitz. It will be hard enough moving around in this fucking costume. Why don't we just shoot each other, and put ourselves out of our misery?"

"Don't tempt me, Handy. Don't tempt me." Fitzsimmons was only half-joking.

Oily gutter water grease-sprayed a forlorn poodle outside Harry's Venice studio. Cody cackled as he coasted to a stop five yards ahead of the snarling mutt. "Dumb fucking dog. You'd think it would've learned its lesson by now. Right, Harry?"

He pawed at the signal turner, which activated the eroded windshield wipers, smearing the shield with a grease streak. "I've always wanted to turn one of those ugly yapping bastards into a wet mop."

Harry was unresponsive, his mouth gaping, his freckles suddenly bright on his pale, pink-tinged face. He had drunk himself into utter oblivion, and was semi-conscious, hearing only snippets of Cody's exhaustive monologue.

Cody was triumphant. "I'm the elephant, the caboose. No, that's not what I meant to say. Too much trouble in paradise, even a smudge on my face. Nah. I'll leave the acting to you, Harry. But I ought to smack you. You smoked all the fucking dope."

Harry flinched slightly, but only in response to yet another lone poodle yap. He did not awake.

Cody provided a quick recap of the hacienda fiesta. "Guerrero lasted pretty long. I thought the skinny bastard couldn't compete with you, but he almost caught you sleeping with that first slap. Must have some Russian blood in you or something. Hey, man, I'm planning on bringing Jen down for you. You don't look good. If a slap won't wake you up, maybe her body will. I heard she gave up on all the pills, too, so she likes to screw again."

Harry picked his right nostril with his right pinky, but did not respond. Air faintly spluttered his lips. His yawn was deep and long.

Cody's voice keened. "Tell me, why did you have to do that? Joaquin will never be able to show his face again down there. You weren't supposed to beat Guerrero in a drinking and bitch slap game..."

"It's not a 'bitch slap game,' as you so unceremoniously call it. It's an honor-bound tradition." Harry's eyes remained closed. "You don't have the faintest idea what's involved."

"Sorry, Mr. Resident Genius, but I don't see it that way. You were a fucking sloppy drunk." Cody gestured toward the dog. "Or, as I see it, no better than a wet, mangy mutt."

Harry's eyes finally opened. "No, I wasn't. How did I prevail then? I had to show him I was superior. Ay, there's the rub."

Cody opened his squeaking door. "That's your problem then. Anyway, I need to take a nap for a while, then go out and get laid."

"Suit yourself. I'll just sleep here a while." The poodle shook-sprayed the grimy water onto the soiled front fender. Harry interpreted the sound as the cascading waterfall in his own Garden of Eden.

For the ballistics extravaganza on the parade ground, a motion picture specialist had been brought in to consult the police carpenter/maintainer on the stylized cutouts of cardboard criminals. He used the flowing red scarf around his bullish neck as the handkerchief to wipe away tears that beset him when his lumpish form was targeted by prying eyes, sometimes popping yet another valium that his gurgling stomach could barely contain, because he was hypersensitive about his own jiggling flesh. To offset his own anxiety, he cursed often, and his obscenities were laced with glee:

"Hey, that looks like a flamer, asshole! Don't paint red lips on a cowboy! And get rid of the stubble and cigars from those blockheads! Christ! Doesn't the police department have one original sketch artist?"

His constant pacing provoked Chief Bender to draw Agent Crum back to the makeshift trailer headquarters, which already had a fine coating of dust, and a distinctive reek inside, where they finished off a bottle of Wild Turkey. Meanwhile, the parking lot a hundred yards or so back beyond the grassless knoll began to fill. The skinny parking attendant in white pants and yellow shirt absented himself momentarily behind a gnarly tree to imbibe off his brimming flask, returning with an annoying burr in his sock.

O'Dool returned to a spot at the furthest remove from the parade ground, conspicuously attended by a pot boiler paperback book; which he pleasantly found readable. Once the event concluded, he planned to scour the Police Records Hall for information on the 'Billy Boy' affair. He then expected Marie to demand that he take off consecutive days from work in order to properly commiserate with her. He fanned the book and appreciatively ran his fingers along the yellowing, slightly rough pages. He arched his eyebrows when a flowery parasol wielded by a sashaying spinster almost dislodged the book from his hands.

"Oh, goodness. I am quite sorry, young man. Am I excused?" Her chin upturned slightly, and her upper lip stretched toward the button nose. Her left hand pulled at the satiny dress fabric at her hips with a rigid grip.

"Of course, ma'am. No harm done." O'Dool turned his head away before she could exploit the opening to ask about the status of the seat next to him. He continued to read while Chief Bender assailed the crowd with his prepared speech:

"Ladies and gentlemen, welcome to the first Annual O.K. Corral Shootout. You will be entertained by our foremost expert marksmen of the world-renowned LAPD. This is a demonstration of the passion and dash and, I must admit, true esprit of my subordinates. Notice their authentic old west costumes, people. And, remember, the one lucky person with the correct raffle ticket will be able to join them after the event for a camp side lunch of franks and beans. Now, without further ado, let the event begin!"

Bender cringed, because Fitzsimmons and Hernandez came out goose-stepping like WWII soldiers of the German Wehrmacht, even giving the Sieg Heil salute. Flatulence, cheers, and jeers burst from the crowd. O'Dool thought it a bizarre corollary to the Mexico fiasco and, despite himself, admired Fitz's twisted drama. O'Dool realized that he was behind the transgression of decorum, because "Nazi" was a word that had been spread through the local press in the recent past, adding to Bender's concern about the upcoming mayoral election. Thus, Fitz was taking advantage of a politically opportune moment.

Bender held the microphone away from his face and muttered under his breath, "I'll get you bastards yet. Just see."

In front of the Police Records building, with its drab, gray exterior, like an old, decommissioned battleship, O'Dool curbed the car next to a catering truck, whose shining mud flaps advertised nude women. Maria flitted through O'Dool's mind like the proverbial jalapeno pepper, then the belch from the truck returned him to noxious contemplation of wife Marie.

He felt extremely weary, even though the ballistics charade had merely been a pretext to log more overtime hours. And, despite Bender's chagrin, the crowd had reveled in the old west histrionics, clamoring for some sort of encore. Finally, Bender had obliged them by commandeering a horse-drawn covered wagon, compelling Hernandez and Fitzsimmons to dive away into the dust with life-affirming haste. Something about the spectacle had prompted O'Dool to visit Marie's taco stand while Fitzsimmons cursed, sat up, and emptied his boots in front of the delighted crowd. Of course, Marie had to do nothing more than exchange pleasantries in order for O'Dool's infatuation to increase.

O'Dool shrugged as he clambered onto the curb and checked the parking meter, straining to understand the Spanish exchanged between the catering truck customers. He hurried across the open lawn, and ducked into the lobby, because the sun was glaring, bringing the slants of shade into stark relief, the monolithic, mason building appearing like a gigantic castle of sand in the Pacific Ocean. He flashed his shield, and was granted access to the elevators, where he reassuringly patted the heaviness of his gun.

His nose latched on the faint odor of Pall Mall tobacco inside the steel cage, a label that Fitzsimmons had recently begun to favor. Still, he was loathe to pull the gun out of the holster, since he could not be sure that the file room was empty, and he did not want to cause undue panic.

His feet almost slipped on the recent application of wax, and the whirring of a fan made him suspect the presence of someone. But he quickly navigated the large rows of gray file cabinets to determine that it was, indeed, empty. Then it was only a matter of scanning the vast stores of the closed files for the letter "T." He quickly discovered the tab: File Removed. Palm Desert Police Records. Per F.

The authorization signature read "Manley," the chief records clerk, but O'Dool only had to compare them to three other index cards to determine that it was a forgery. But why remove them to another county? He sat wearily, and wondered if he should examine other files for possible forgery and/or theft. After he had paced back and forth to the windows a couple of times, he replaced the file folder and emptied a stale coffee pot. "What exactly was the Billy Boy business, Fitz?" he said aloud, and found the elevator.

He ascended the steps slowly, noting the immaculate condition of the rosebushes and ice plants and cacti. They had been recently groomed with the feminine care that Marie lorded over him. Already, he could sense her admonishing him, "You insensitive fool." Still, after a momentary pause, he took the steps two at a time, only hesitating at the last flight, where he could espy her smoking and reading on the balcony. It was still difficult not to marvel at her severe form of beauty, the sharp lines of jaw and nose, her legs long and thin, still shapely for her age. It reminded him of the first time he had seen her, from the back of a line at a police management seminar, staring at her feet housed in high heels.

Before he could retrieve a Tab from the refrigerator, she was upon him. "I see that you don't care anymore about calling ahead."

"What?"

She motioned circles with a pointed finger. "Dialing a phone, that's what I'm talking about. You haven't exactly made any effort to be considerate towards me."

"Marie, a lot has happened with work lately."

"What's new about that? Don't use it as an excuse. If you had allowed yourself to be promoted, perhaps you wouldn't be too busy to worry about being a husband." She tapped ashes onto the flower linoleum countertop for the first time.

"Okay, Marie. I won't argue with you. I'm ready to quit. I'm tired of being a stool pigeon for so-called public protection."

"Now, don't cynical, honey. I didn't mean to say that your profession is dishonorable. You think in terms of black-and-white…"

"Like a cop?" O'Dool chewed a piece of ice from his glass of Tab.

"Stop blaming everything on your job. You know there is counseling for that. Anyway, you haven't lost a partner yet, and you haven't had to…"

O'Dool's frustration continued to mount. "You mean kill anyone, Marie. No, I haven't. But I've seen people bleed to death and bodies hacked apart and women battered until they're unrecognizable. I've…"

Marie's voice became cutting. "Okay, you've made your point. You've told me a bit about it in the past. But can we afford you quitting now? I mean, I'd rather move back to Chicago than live here in this bungalow. Wait until things blow over before you make a rash decision. I'm still too young to live off my family's wealth."

O'Dool's tone was curt. "That's honorable of you, Marie. But who's been working all these years?"

"Listen, honey, if you want to crawl back to Chicago with me, okay, but I'll be the one in charge. And if you want to stay out here and chase young women with your free time, don't expect me to support that habit. My family's wealth will not be frittered away by whoring."

"Enough!" O'Dool snapped. "I'm packing my suitcase for Palm Springs. I have business to take care of there. When I get back I promise we'll talk more about it."

Marie's voice dripped with sarcasm. "What is 'it,' honey? What you can seduce with charm and dash?"

"No. 'Our life,' as you call it."

"Well, at least now you're making sense." She stubbed out the cigarette on the counter and sashayed back to the balcony, where a squirrel abandoned his spying post. "Just don't be surprised if I'm gone when you get back," she said.

It was near dusk. Harry's Volkswagen van spluttered north on the PCH, his neck pink-tinged from the sun slanting off the ocean. He had shrugged off Cody's petulant appeal to be driven up to Tuna Canyon for the trailer party, despite Cody's promise to bring Jen along as long as Harry volunteered to pick her up at Union Station downtown and brave comments directed at one greasy gringo. He had a tall Budweiser can between his legs and a pre-wrapped marijuana joint in his jean jacket pocket, exclaiming to the salty air, "There will be other mermaid broads up in the hills. Sure."

Halfway up the winding road, he pulled off at a turn-out to relieve himself. A momentary jolt of vertigo as he peered down between the cliffs made him think of the time Bruce had suspended Cody above the chasm. Cody had almost squirmed free, but to his death, when one of his shoes came off in Harry's hands. Bruce had relented, "Aw, we'll let the little sewer rat live a little longer."

He parked at the point where the dirt driveway bisected the asphalt road, in a slight depression that was gloaming with the pink fire of the sunset. He heard the echoes of some rock music, and saw the rippling of the boys in the underbrush, chasing Reed.

Dr. Aziz stealthily approached Harry from behind, placing his cocktail glass in his wife Amina's hand, and slowly wound his way through the jostling crowd outside the candlelit trailer. "Like a cobra," he thought, his right arm reaching out to tap the shoulder from behind.

"I sensed your presence, Dr. Aziz," Harry said without turning, winking at Dan, who was in the process of perfecting the roach-clipped joint.

"I saw his presence, Harry." Dan said it a severe tone, like an Indian medicine man.

Harry said, "You're a fucking asshole, man. No, I'm not addressing you, Aziz. This freak is happy because he finished his construction job, so he can devote himself again to art full-time. He had to run it out for the poor boss of his who was looking stressed to death. Obviously under some sort of severe pressure to finish quickly, but…"

Aziz relented, and circled around to face them both. He noticed that Harry, wearing his dark sweater (the easier to admit various food stains) smirked at his yellow cardigan. Dan smiled wisely.

Aziz coughed dramatically. "May I ask what is your excuse?"

"For what?" Harry's chest expanded.

"For not being productive with your artwork?" He saw Amina chatting with Sara in the background.

"I have no excuse, but neither do I need one. I create when I must, that's all. Most times I'd rather watch those Charlie's Angels broads parade across the screen." Harry giggled.

"I see," Aziz nodded patronizingly. "So, you only create when you must. And your meditation is soft pornography and such…"

Harry chirped, "Yeah, it's like dropping a log, when you have to, there's no avoiding it."

Aziz's nose upturned, as if he had caught a scent from the Cagao, the sacred Spanish God of Defecation. His eyes took in the boys circling the open fire, watching the pig sizzle on the spit, with Reed supervising from the lawn chair, throwing in kindling wood from time to time. "So you wait for the signal? I understand. That must be why you avoid me visiting your studio."

Harry stared at the fire. "Dr. Aziz, perhaps you should consider that that I do not respond to those who want me to justify, whether it be myself or my artwork. Notice that I never describe any of my work in detail."

"Yes, it's as if, Harry, that you hold yourself above the pleasant exchanges exchanged between…"

"Hey, guys," Dan interjected, "no need to argue a debatable point."

Harry rejoined, "Aziz, you cling to traditional aesthetics. I admit they are admirable, but well-trodden all the same. You lack an appreciation for infinity."

Aziz's voice sounded distant. "Far from it. I see those fire sparks merging with eternity."

"How poetic! Ah! But pure hogwash. All I see is a suckling pig being roasted for our enjoyment. See how I turn the tables, so to speak?" Harry fairly crowed.

"Harry, you incorrigible monkey, I only demand your best work. Can't you see that I'm challenging your muse, not you?" Aziz had usurped the mantle of authority.

Harry paused to consider. "Okay, okay, Aziz, I guess you've got me by the balls there, as women put my balls in a noose." He winked at the fire.

"Pardon?" Aziz grimaced, which showed how unnaturally large his mouth was in comparison to an otherwise thin face.

Harry shrugged. "Never mind. Don't you guys like the look of that fire? I'm going out to see which of my faces I can find in it." He knelt down beside Reed, patted his shoulder, and smiled. Reed smiled back, and the boys kept running.

CHAPTER 20

O'Dool's out of town sojourns had been limited to his strained flights to the in-laws in Chicago, fascinated by nothing more than the building block Sears Tower under construction, and the sleek John Hancock monolith of black steel. Marie's father Chuck had engineered an efficient relationship with him, modeled on the merits of architecturally sound, and dynamic development. O'Dool grew tired of the constant tight steering at the dinner table toward design dilemmas, and would escape to a dingy bar inside the Loop district when Marie, a notoriously hard sleeper, went to bed. Sometimes O'Dool drove down to the lake and walked through Grant Park, nipping off a whiskey flask. There were hobos nestled in sleeping blankets who, noticing his bulky and confident form, whispered "undercover" and "narc" to each other.

In the morning, Chuck insisted on including him in discussions about floor plans, materials, and potential cost, until O'Dool hid behind the Sports section of the morning paper and nursed a bitter cup of coffee, watching rain outside the foggy window turn to sleet. Meanwhile, he thought, "Yeah, I admire some of your city's skyscrapers. But that doesn't mean I want to learn your chosen trade."

O'Dool took the on-ramp at excessive speed, slowing ratcheting back his foot pressure on the pedal as he merged into the fast lane behind a Camaro, splotchy from its recent primer coating. For the first time, he actively wondered about Marie. He had always prized her loyalty, but there was also an unyielding and rigid side to her character. Even her passion, when it came, seemed prearranged. Then he turned the radio volume up to try to distance himself, and crept up on the Camaro until he could see the tread on the wide tires, and the annoyed glance in the rearview mirror, the small head on the spindly neck jerking into profile. He felt vaguely threatened. The youngish image reminded him of Billy Thompson, and his cocksure way with women.

About an hour later, he noticed the young driver awkwardly holding some sort of map in front of his face, and wondered how far it would take him. "Should have run while you still had the chance, Billy," he said aloud. When he passed the huge field of wind propellers near Palm Springs, he wondered if he should have applied to aeronautics school afterall. At the time, his parents were preparing to sell the failing machine shop, and urged a solid, safe career, rather than one filled with numerous risks.

He drove directly to the Hall of Records building, situated behind the squat, sprawling, ranch-like Palm Desert County courthouse, framed by blooming birds-of-paradise, fronds slowly opening like the green mouths of pelicans. Even at this time, in early September, the desert mountains had a fine chaff of snow atop their peaks. O'Dool recalled taking Marie up on the tram for their first honeymoon, and the strange experience of witnessing light snowfall in desert mountains.

He flashed his badge, and was immediately granted entrance. The receptionist wore the slightly smeared lipstick look that Marie abhorred. "Good day," she remarked.

"You too." As soon as he was beyond the first hallway, he moved his right hand closer to his shoulder holster, brushing past the defunct posters of Wanted Hell's Angels.

The file had been removed, with no signature reference. He briefly considered asking the receptionist about Fitzsimmons, then resigned himself to scouring local hotels and motels for a likely inebriated older bachelor.

It was only the fifth hotel he had checked, yet there it was, a cream yellow Cadillac, the motel flood lights blaring off the gigantic hood, the whitewall tires shiny with a recent coat of protectant. He parked across the street, and put his hand on the hood, which was not even lukewarm, and quickly glanced through the finely sandblasted windows, which only revealed some fast food wrappings. He looked at the curb, and the space of adjacent spaces, but none were numbered. The light in the room facing the car was on.

He retreated back to his car to consider his next step. He felt that he could immediately confront Fitzsimmons, or wait for another opportune time, perhaps at a familiar bar somewhere back in L.A., even on the Sunset strip, Fitz's favorite haunt. But the cooled hood of the car indicated that it had not been driven for quite some time, pointing toward its driver being relaxed, or even asleep. "Get him while he's slow," he thought.

He knocked once, and tried to gain a peek, but the powder blue curtains were drawn tightly, allowing only a soft gauze of yellow light. Balling his hand, he punched once, twice, fairly certain that the resulting thud would not disturb the neighbors.

"Yeah, what do you want?" The voice sounded unusually nasal, but there could be no mistaking who it belonged to.

O'Dool adopted a slight accent. "Senor, I have complimentary cigarros. I sell door to door and…"

"Go away, amigo. You sound desperate to me." Fitzsimmons hurriedly put on a pair of dark slacks and a v-neck white t-shirt, and slowly approached the door, his holstered gun still indenting the mildewy lounge chair about teen feet behind him.

O'Dool strained forward. "Senor, just un momentito, por que…"

"What? Go away, amigo. I don't like having to tell you twice." Fitz looked back briefly at the gun resting on the lounge chair.

O'Dool gauged the volume of the voice and its relation to the door, then stepped back and kicked. His foot punched through the cheap, fiber board, but it held.

"Hey, amigo, are you a soccer player or something?" Fitzsimmons' voice was booming, but a bit more distant, and O'Dool hesitated, because a retreat seemed prudent and yet unadvised, because he could not imagine reaching his car before Fitzsimmons identified him.

This time he led with his shoulder. He splintered the door into two large pieces, one still locked in the frame. On his way to the floor, he sensed a shape to his left, and threw out his leg. The form was unsettled, and dropped to the ground. He rolled back to his knees, and leveled the gun at Fitzsimmons, who was struggling to turn over.

"Just as I figured, Fitz. Caught you after a couple of cocktails." Standing, he backed away to the door with his badge already produced from his pocket. He flashed it at a young woman and her son at the end of the carport, and called out, "Go back inside. Police business." Then, with his gun still trained on his fallen colleague, he dragged the pieces of the door and propped them up against the door jamb.

"Cheap fuckin' door, huh, Fitz?" O'Dool told himself to not be complacent, even though he had the upper hand.

Fitzsimmons blurted, "Are you insane? What are you doing here? And what's with the suicide charge? You were lucky to graze me, because I would've hit you in the chest. I guess you forgot about me besting Handy at the range."

O'Dool parried, "I figured you would be just slow enough for that not to happen. Just a tad sloppy. I saw your burger wrappings so I knew you might be greasy slow."

"You are fucking insane." Fitzsimmons again gazed at his pistol, just out of reach, and moved to sit on the edge of the bed, without swaying much. "I don't know what you're thinking, but I never betrayed you, because you're so fucking likable."

O'Dool was unmoved. "Never mind about that. I just want to know about what happened to Billy."

Fitzsimmons smiled ungenerously. "Ah, I see. You're looking for the file. But I won't give it to you. First, you have no jurisdiction over the case."

O'Dool snapped. "Don't give me that crap. Anyway, I'd just like to know what happened." O'Dool leaned back against the dresser and lowered the weapon to his thigh.

Fitzsimmons took a deep breath. "Look, a long time ago Billy Thompson was the first to come on the scene of a fatal bike wreck. Some alcohol was involved, although the officer had ridden at a more intoxicated level in the past. A beautiful girl, who the bachelor cop really loved, was killed. Billy made a deal, that he would not report all the details, even gave him some gum to cover up the cop's intoxication, and agreed that the cop could clean up the mess on his own. In exchange, well, Billy Boy would be taken under his wing and some small misdemeanor nonsense erased from his past so he could fulfill his dream of becoming a cop. Pretty far out, right?"

"I gather then, Fitz, that at a later point in time, Billy was for some reason threatening to turn you in?" O'Dool shifted slightly, and peered toward the door to make sure no gawkers had appeared. The yellow light was fairly streaming through the splintered door.

"Bravo, Doolie. You pick it up fast. No wonder, well, yeah. You see, it sounds crazy, but it all came down to boots." Fitzsimmons stared at his own bare feet and for the first and last time sounded slightly ashamed.

"What? Get to the point, or I might change my mind about that file."

Fitzsimmons raised his chin. "Okay. I don't know why Billy wanted Betsy's boots. It was like he wanted them to show that he got the better end of the bargain, I guess. Or, maybe to use as evidence against me. He wouldn't stop bringing them up, even though my warnings became more and more serious."

O'Dool's tone was derisive. "So you killed him over a pair of boots."

"Fuck you. What right did he have to them anyway? A snot-nosed kid from the valley wearing those nerdy striped t-shirts, I helped him become the man women loved, then he wants to undermine me and drop hints about turning me in for asking for a fucking pair of boots?"

O'Dool was squinting through the shaft of light, and heard the drone of a small plane overhead. "But why those particular pair of boots, Fitz? Couldn't you have given him another pair?"

O'Dool was insistent. "No. He had pictures taken of them, even had them numbered inside with an awl. That's how obsessed he became with them. He got weird about it. He would start saying, "I want the Betsys. Pathological, right?"

"You're lying." O'Dool raised his gun again.

"No, I'm not. That kid became spoiled by all the attention. Some people lose their heads in bright lights. They get paralyzed by obsession. You know what I'm talking about."

"Yes, but then why didn't you just give them to him?" O'Dool was incredulous.

"No! Betsy was my girl. You know the few you never forget, and not just the young ones that died? She could have made me better. She didn't try to keep a hold over me with her sex like other women. She was pure in her own way. Not perfect, but never put on an act. You know how rare that is, don't you? Men kill for that. And I was responsible for her death. I was in a daze, but I couldn't help it. I unzipped her boots and pulled them off, one sticky with her blood. Those boots have reminded me of what I lost, but also what I keep, the memory of her."

"So you pulled them off her body?" O'Dool was aghast.

Fitzsimmons was almost whimpering. "Yeah, so what? You think it's sick. I like you, but you're fucking naïve sometimes."

"So you had him killed?" O'Dool said rhetorically. "As if that could erase your guilt? Look, Fitz, you should have got rid of the boots. You ever think of burning them?"

Fitzsimmons ran his hand across the acrylic quilt. "Never. You're not driving at what I think you are, are you? Look at it this way, if he hadn't come around that corner that night, I could've cleaned up the mess myself."

O'Dool retorted, "Yeah, but someone else might not have kept quiet, either."

"Right! We both did each other favors. But if I'd known how conniving the prick would become, I never would've gotten mixed up with him. Should've shot the bastard…"

O'Dool's gun hand was slightly shaking. "He saved your career and…"

Fitzsimmons' hand clenched the quilt. "Bullshit. Even if I'd fessed up it wouldn't have gone beyond probation. But let's go back a little in time. I've got a story that will help you understand the complete picture. We can go back in time together, O'Dool, since we started on the force around the same time. You remember the Safeway robbery, right?"

"Yeah, Diana Carrillo was one of the star witnesses. But I guess you conveniently forgot about that when you had her offed."

"Let me tell you another side of the whole story, all right? But lower the gun a bit, all right? You're making me nervous."

O'Dool shrugged, and kept the gun pointed, but on its side in his lap. "Go ahead, but I doubt you can convince me of anything."

"March 12, 1967. Light showers all day. Picked up my first Caddie, the black one, 0700 sharp. New tires kept my cornering tight. Was at Rampart for maybe fifteen minutes when the call came in. Robbery in progress. Venice Blvd. - Sawtelle Safeway. Shots fired. Shotguns taken out of the closets. Some dumb rookies took out patrol cars without properly checking the numbers, so had to rev up my Caddie instead. When we arrived, Captain Turnbow from the Hollywood precinct was in charge, an intense ex-narc, and artillery officer in the Pacific War, had greasy hair and a pockmarked face, a little gung-ho even by Rampart's standards. Since the shots, it had been quiet inside the building. Not much store activity before the incident because during a shift change. Turnbow quickly on the bullhorn trying to make contact, but no response."

"Quickly, he pulled all the officers into a circle, and told us eyewitnesses had not seen any cars leave the lot, no one on foot, either. He had us form a perimeter around the building, with the larger group under Pride and Cheadle going to the back service entrance, while us and Mankins and Treadwell were charged with going in directly from the front. Treadwell made everyone nervous. Remember? Former Green Beret in 'Nam still in his twenties, had muttonchops. Always looked casual, but the kind of guy who wanted to kick a door down even if he could simply turn the door knob instead. Then Mankins, the old-timer with the porkpie hat. The lifer. Almost killed by a bullet, could have accepted a cushy pension, but decided to continue on instead. Turnbow escorted us to the front entrance and told us to ferry info back to him when the situation changed. A SWAT copter arrived overhead the same time as an annoying little rain squall. Turnbow saluted it and walked ahead.

O'Dool briefly interrupted. "So we were on the flanks going in? Is that how you remember it?"

"Yeah, basically, I guess our versions might be slightly different inside. By the way, did you ever hear that Bender kept SWAT back intentionally for a while? Yeah, heard he told Smitty later that year that he had confidence in us without that backup, that he knew we would be fine, but I doubt that. Anyway, Turnbow came jogging up and said he'd finally received info that there had been a biker gang circling around the building earlier that morning, who parked their bikes in an abandoned lot, and were seen climbing the chain link fence behind the Safeway service area. Apparently we were dealing with Hells Angels."

"The first thing I noticed inside was some blood between the end of an aisle and a checkout counter. Smeared like ketchup, really. Then I thought I heard a cough before I realized it was a cranky ceiling fan. Boxes and cans on the floor, as if people had raked them off the shelves on their way to the back. Even though we moved slowly and cautiously, not wanting to overlook anything, it was clear all the trouble was in back. Treadwell waited for us to enter the commercial area with him, his eyes on fire, and that's when we heard the first voices. Weird scene. Then a body came flying out through the opening, and almost collided with Treadwell. It was the body of the store manager, the chest stained with blood. We barely had time to consider it before the grenade came rolling out."

"We dove in all directions. When I came to, it was clear Mankins had run out of luck, I crawled over and found you still had a pulse. That crazy bastard Treadwell had actually gone forward, and I found him shot, but alive, close to two dead bikers. He was cursing at me, "What're you looking at? They've got a girl and a bundle of cash. So stop looking at me, looks worse than it is. Get out of here!" There was not any blood coming from his mouth, so I ran out the back. First thing I noticed was another two bikers down at the back, and cops climbing over the fence to get to the adjacent parking lot."

O'Dool pointed the gun more directly again. "Okay, I've got it. You flagged down one of the pursuing cars, and the chase began. So cut to the chase then, Fitz."

Fitzsimmons' faced turned red and his arms tightened, then loosened. "Okay. Okay. They had Diana Carrillo, and we were in pursuit south on Venice Blvd. Somehow, Treadwell got on Turnbow's radio and said, 'Waste all the greaseballs," before he was cut off. Being on bikes, they had an advantage of swerving around southbound traffic, but we kept pace. There were six bikers left. When we got to Abbot Kinney near the ocean, I told the driver to clip them. He looked at me kind of funny, and I yelled, "Cut them off, goddamnit! Then I'll clip them!" He accelerated, but I could tell he was still unsure, so I yelled, "Hold on!" and wrenched the wheel to the right. Sounded like a bomb had gone off when we collided. We spun, and bodies and bikes were flying through the air. When we finally settled after all the chaos, we were unhurt, but a couple of bikers were crawling, moaning, and screaming in pain. One was crumpled around a telephone pool in a huge pool of blood, but Diana looked amazingly okay beyond a mere facial bruise, although I realized…"

O'Dool interrupted. "The collision was intentional? You could've easily killed Diana, too, and…"

"Yeah, pissed me off. So much that before the paramedics arrived I acted like I was trying to revive a biker chick, but, actually, I was slowly suffocating her. I can't stand tough, butch chicks. Of course, I made sure my cop driver and Diana didn't see it. He was shook up big-time."

"Diana was easy to get in the sack after that. I told her we had hit a small pothole in the road, and that's why we had swerved toward them. That punk Billy Thompson later went with her to discover that there was never a hole in the road to speak of. Just another reason I had to waste both of them."

"Damn, Fitz, your sadism is contagious. Makes we want to shoot your kneecaps off. I just can't quite do it. You're too fucking pathetic. You should've been the one to get the force of the grenade, not the old codger Mankins. You have to be on the stage, or you squall like a baby. Somehow you want to impress me still, but it's over. You view your reputation as more vital than other people's lives. You were protecting your rep, and for that you viewed Billy's life expendable."

"Billy was exploiting my goodwill, stealing my girlfriends." Fitzsimmons' eyes scanned the blank walls.

'Who didn't love you to begin with…"

"Fuck you!" Fitzsimmons shot a glance at his gun five feet away. "You know how close you came to dying through your stunt? Just because I was at a vulnerable moment."

"Yeah, so I calculated. Fuck, Fitz, it all started with Betsy. You wanted to break the chain by killing Billy instead of burning a material pair of boots. You could not kill him personally because, deep down, you knew it wasn't justified. So, instead, you hire some eses from East L.A. It also means you didn't love any of those girlfriends like you claim. You're like Bender and Crum. No, they're sociopaths. You're an outright psychopath."

Fitzsimmons' head jerked just perceptibly, as if he had seen something outside. Suddenly his voice was calm. "Huh?"

"Why did you sign off with your initial-'per F'? Huh? And why didn't you pull the departmental scent off the Lobos and Locos rendezvous? It's like you've been entrapping yourself."

"Okay, gumshoe. Or should I call you a sanctimonious monk instead? You have an ice queen for a wife, everyone can see it but you, but you still refuse to have a good time with all the horny young girls from bumfuck Iowa. That's insane."

"Back to the subject, Fitz." O'Dool thought he saw a shadow beyond the edge of the parking lot, because he was in the space of the disintegrated door.

"All right, all right. I had to get rid of both of them to clear my trail, even Diana Carrillo. She had the nerve to try to blackmail me, too. And who were they anyway? Just a couple of party freaks that even Bender and other police brass realized had to be gotten rid of. And offing him in the desert was beautiful, the Lobos found a full-blooded Mescalero Apache just back from Vietnam, a stone cold killer. He fucking broke Billy Boy's neck with his bare hands, although he's quite a shot from a distance, I might add. I've got my own contacts in these parts, men with hot Apache blood. And they still enjoy popping Palefaces. I'm just another of Bender's tentacles. He's even involved with construction unions now. His pulse ran in my blood long before you started picking up scents. Yeah, you heard me right. Bender's tight with the mob, too. Now you look surprised. But why? Haven't you ever considered that you're the moth being drawn to my flame?" He stood up and, while O'Dool's finger moved to the trigger, waved his hand at the opening.

O'Dool felt the paralyzing bullet above his heart. But because his finger was already on the trigger, he was was able to fire one shot at Fitzsimmons.

Fitzsimmons slumped to the floor, made a few spluttering noises, then was silent. O'Dool's right leg pistoned out and made the last, splintered remains of the door fall. He waited, straining to look into the distance while still seated. But a second shot did not follow the first from the nearby mesa.

O'Dool blinked, but the revealed image would not fade, until it bled into nothingness: an Apache warrior with a red headband, rifle slung across his back, retreated through prickly pear, ocotillo, and saguaro cacti.

O'Dool thought, "he's in no hurry," and expired.

www.ingramcontent.com/pod-product-compliance
Lightning Source LLC
Chambersburg PA
CBHW030531030726
47495CB00004B/948